Always, Clementine

Carlie Sorosiak

WALKER BOOKS

Text copyright © 2022 by Carlie Sorosiak
Illustrations copyright © 2022 by Vivienne To
Epigraph copyright © 1963 from *The Bell Jar* by Sylvia Plath

First US edition 2022
Also published by Nosy Crow (UK) 2022

Library of Congress Catalog Card Number 2021953115
ISBN 978-1-5362-2884-7

22 23 24 25 26 27 LBM 10 9 8 7 6 5 4 3 2 1

Printed in Melrose Park, IL, USA

This book was typeset in Libre Baskerville.

Walker Books US
a division of
Candlewick Press
99 Dover Street
Somerville, Massachusetts 02144

www.walkerbooksus.com

A JUNIOR LIBRARY GUILD SELECTION

For all the lab animals,
past and present

I took a deep breath and listened
to the old brag of my heart:
I am, I am, I am.

—Sylvia Plath, *The Bell Jar*

Chess is life in miniature.

—attributed to Garry Kasparov

Part I
Openings

Letter 1

Dear Rosie,

There once was a mouse. That's me. Hello!

As you can probably tell, I'm not sure how to begin. This is my first time writing a letter. And it's not even writing! It's more like thinking. I am *thinking* a letter.

This would be so much easier if I could just see your face: your white chin whiskers, your amber eyes. Did you know that one hundred minutes have passed since we last spoke? You probably do.

Let me start again. My brain is firing in many, many directions—and it's hard to concentrate my thoughts. This often happens. I will focus them here. Inside a mailbox.

Rosie, I'm stuck inside a mailbox!

Sound it out with your fingers. *Mail-box.* It's a place where people deposit their letters, their ideas, their wishes for one another. In this mailbox, every letter is addressed to the same person. The envelopes smell of paper and taste like—wait a second—oh, they do not taste good. (*Pew!* I'm spitting them out now.)

Despite everything that's just happened to me, Rosie, I am an optimist. A very difficult thing to be, sometimes, at three inches tall. But my tail is still curling at the *boom-boom-boom* of thunder outside. Oh! It's so shaky! So loud! All I can do is tuck myself into the shadow of a letter, looking up to see—yes, that's interesting, the stamp is exactly the size of my head.

Are you afraid?

Are you missing me, too?

How long before I see you again?

As I'm tucking, as I'm tail-curling, I'm trying to figure out a way back to you. We've never been apart for this long. I am your mouse. You are my chimpanzee. Will you be taller, seconds or minutes or days from now? Will you still let me climb onto your shoulder, up the black hair of your arm? I like that! I like how you laugh when I press my paws to your nose.

Until then, I'll write these letters. *Think* these letters. That way, when you lift me into the bare palm of your hand again, all my memories will be right there. And I can tell you everything.

(If I'm not gone forever first.)

Always,

Clementine

Letter 2

Dear Rosie,

It has been seventeen seconds since my last letter. How are you?

Rain is hammering the mailbox! This mailbox is supposed to help protect me. Protect me from what, I do not know. But each *rap* and *drop* of rain prickles my fur. My tail stiffens.

Thunder is the second-loudest noise I've ever heard.

We'll get to the first later. Right now, considering that I'm stuck (and not afraid!), I'd like to busy my brain. Shouldn't we start at the beginning? I was planning on telling you this someday! My origins. My life before you. I don't know yours, so I'd like you—at least—to know mine.

I remember the day I was born. Maybe this is strange, to remember the exact moment you entered the world. But I do. It was warm, wood shavings were soft around me, and I thought to myself: *Breathe.*

Then I thought: *Prime numbers are asymptomatically*

distributed among positive integers, and light travels propor-
tionally through the vacuum of space.

More interesting ideas would come.

Keep in mind, though, I didn't have any fur yet. My eyes hadn't opened. My ears—small and velvety pink—couldn't hear a single noise. That's why it took me twenty-five days (plus or minus seven seconds) to discover that I was the smartest mouse in history.

"She could be the smartest mouse in history," said one of the researchers. That was a clue. As was the fact that I understood human language. The other lab mice didn't follow conversations the way I did. They didn't sit dreamily at the edge of our cage, forepaws tucked under their chins, and just listen.

Different. I wasn't *sure* I was different. How can you really know? You can't ask the other mice, *When you're drinking from that water bottle, are you solving equations at the same time? If you dream at night, is it in Latin? Do you have a thinking cap (a miniature pom-pom from a human's sweater)?*

No.

We cuddled in a pile. We played. Our fur grew in at the same time. I have a heart-shaped spot, just above my tail, and so did one of the other mice. A lab is a place for scientific tests, and we were all a big part of those tests; yet, in most ways, we seemed unalike. My cage-mates peered at me strangely as I threw myself into activities. Waiting around, waiting for the next part of the experiment, is uninteresting. So I saved all my food pellets in the corner of the cage, hiding them beneath the water bottle, then stuffed them in my mouth—all at once. I developed theories about how far my cheeks could balloon. And I noticed that the harder I thought, the more my fur smelled of raspberries. (Apparently this was a side effect of the experiment. Although the rest of the mice just smelled like mice.)

Wait! What was that noise? That noise, right now? Is someone outside the mailbox? Is that a tree branch or a human or just the rain? I lift onto my hind toes, ears vibrating, whiskers whiskering.

Hmm. It's gone.

Now, where was I?

Oh! The maze.

The maze changed everything.

Lab mice are supposed to follow the jumble of trails. I did that—one time. But why go *through* the maze if you can simply . . . leave? Standing on my hind paws, I wobbled a bit, calculated the trajectory, then sprung over the wall, landing with a gentle *thump* on the table.

"Did you see that?" a researcher said, grabbing me.

"See what?" asked another.

"This mouse. She hopped out of the maze like some sort

of pogo stick! None of the others have done that." He lifted me in his palm until he met my stare. My mind was wandering toward electromagnetic waves and the Pythagorean theorem and also brussels sprouts, which are delicious. "Her eyes look so *human*. Don't they look human?"

A human eye is half the size of my body. How odd would I look if my eyes were that large?

And why didn't the humans ever ask *me* questions? Why couldn't we brainstorm the experiment together? The lab was studying how to increase intelligence in mammals by altering our DNA. I had so many ideas to help! Like, miniature lab coats for all of us mice. And brussels sprouts sandwiches every twenty-six minutes. And improved analytics for their statistical models.

"Just run it another time," the first researcher said.

In half a second (so quick! ha! ha-ha-ha!), I was out again.

That night, new questions arrived. *Didn't the maze bore the others? Why were they so intent on burrowing when our cage was solid and could not be burrowed through?*

I was missing something. Some important secret about the world.

It was lonely, Rosie.

I was lonely every day, until the night I met you.

Always,

Clementine

Letter 3

Dear Rosie,

In the mailbox, as I'm thinking this letter, I curl up into the tightest ball possible. The safest ball possible. My eyelids slowly blink with the sound of your name. *Rosie. Rosie.* I miss you.

Do you remember when we met?

Sometimes, as the researchers flicked off the lights in the lab, I'd pick the lock of my cage and tiptoe out. Because I'm a good lab mouse.

Here is what a good lab mouse does.

I taste-test bread in the kitchen, leaving a tiny chewhole in each slice. (Once, I heard a researcher say, "Did someone *bite* my sandwich?" *You're welcome*, I thought, paws under my chin, staring proudly at him. *You're so very welcome*.)

I help the custodian, whose name is Harry. (*You are Harry and I am furry*, I giggled to myself, finishing the card game he left out.)

I hide things around a section of the lab—stubs of pencils, pennies, DNA samples—to heighten the mazelike environment for the researchers.

And finally, a good lab mouse does her best for science. I always do my best. I've always believed I'm part of something greater—that the *world* is greater than I know. So, one night, I decided to explore farther than I ever had. Flinging myself off the lab station, I encountered things I'd never sniffed before: sulfur, flower petals, corn chips. My nose tingled. My paws barely made a sound. Across the tile, around a wastebasket, past the kitchen. (I told you I was good at mazes.)

One more corner, and there you were.

There you were, your fingers curled around the metal bars of your cage. Had you ever seen a mouse before? I'd never seen a chimpanzee. But when our eyes found each other, I knew that I'd discovered someone just as bright as myself. And just as lonely. The wrinkles under your eyes drooped as you gazed in my direction. Whatever you'd asked of me then, Rosie, I would've given it.

But you didn't breathe a word.

I streaked up to you, then stretched my back to peer at your chimp ears, at the magnificent flatness of your face. You smelled large, and sweet like fruit. Like orange slices. Like plums.

Hello!

That's what I mimed. Though you didn't understand, not yet. Amber eyes flickering, your body swayed back and forth. How should a mouse greet a chimpanzee? A long, intense stare, eyes bulging? A series of squeaks? I tried both—and then, optimistically, slipped between the bars. There were no wood shavings like in my cage. Only the cold of metal.

It was so tiny in there.

So tiny, even for a mouse.

Still, you managed to scoop me up. No squirming from me! No ounce of fear. Because *you* didn't pick me up by the tail. That was a clue: You were kind. You were curious. You lifted me softly, until we were eye to eye. Beneath me was the wrinkled skin of your hands, and I shifted my weight from side to side, a prickle of excitement shimmying down my tail. My hindquarters wiggled. *What happens next?* I mused. *And will it involve brussels sprouts?*

(I always wondered if others liked brussels sprouts as much as I do.)

Black hair glittering, you stroked the top of my head with a single finger. Then you pulled me close to your chest, right where your heart was beating. I could tell that your heart was the same size as me, and I thought for a moment: *It's like a mouse is in there.*

9

One ear to your fur, I listened to the *thump*.

And forgot all about vegetables.

That is how we became friends.

(There it is! Another noise! Another noise, outside the mailbox.)

Always,

Clementine

Letter 4

Dear Rosie,

Uncurling from my ball, I sniff. And sniff. The tiniest sliver of air filters into the mailbox, and I perk my sensitive ears.

I can always tell when someone is coming.

My ears always know.

One hundred and two minutes ago, I was with you in your cage. Remember? We'd gotten so used to spending evenings together—and we'd learned to communicate in our own way. It took some effort! I couldn't hoot like a chimpanzee. You couldn't squeak like a mouse. But after a while, you started to mirror my moves. Thoughtfully, I'd scratch my chin. Then you'd scratch yours. You'd show me your play face: mouth wide, jaw hanging open, your bottom teeth a dull white.

Soon, you began speaking with your hands. When I brought you a leftover slice of fruit from a researcher's desk, you signed the word *orange*.

That's an *orange*.

This is an *apple*.

Hello, *orange*, *apple*, *sad*, *home*, *mouse*.

Alongside the alphabet, those are the finger-words you taught me. In return, I lent you my thinking cap. Remember how small it was, compared to your head? You licked the pom-pom, brown nose scrunching in the darkness. Oh! That was so funny! Just so funny. (I think there was a lot of silliness in you, before the lab. If there was a before.)

We could've learned more from each other—but tonight, the lab door swung open.

Footsteps.

Rabbits scrambled in their pens. A beagle howled.

"This is madness," a human said, voice squeaking with anxiety. "But you're going to do this! You *are*. Be brave, be brave, be *brave*. Don't think about all the bad things that could happen . . . Great, now you're thinking about all the bad things that could happen! Stop!" As he rounded the corner, I saw that he was tall. Thin. Much like Felix, the junior researcher. A black mask covered his face and head. Gloves disguised his shaking fingers.

If I'd known . . . if I'd *understood*.

Rosie, I never would've left. I would've tucked myself into the crook of your neck, nestled into your hair, tried my best to disappear. To stay. To be with you! Maybe I could've disguised myself somehow? As a rabbit? Or a guinea pig?

Instead, my nose poked outside your cage. I inched forward. Then traveled toward the commotion. The man was peering into the mouse enclosure, flashlight in hand. "Found you!" he said, lifting one into the air and sniffing his fur. "You have that heart-shaped spot, but you don't smell like raspberries? Maybe you're just . . . not thinking very hard right now? That's it. That must be it. Okay, quick—we're going to have to be so, so, so quick, because otherwise they'll find out, and I'll lose my job, and I'll go to prison—or worse, they'll send me back to *Canada* . . ." He was still squawking to himself when he glimpsed me.

Politely, I waved.

He couldn't seem to process this.

I tried again with my whole body, wiggling—overexaggerating everything. Did he think the mouse in his hands was me? Couldn't be! That mouse is duck-footed! He has an overbite!

"No," the man said. "What?" He shoved the flashlight into his pocket, charged forward, and scooped me up, as he had done with the other mouse. He examined our tails, which are the same, and the heart-shaped spots above our tails, which are the same. "Oh no. Oh no, no. *You're* waving, but how do I know for sure . . . ? Which one is . . . ? Do *you* smell like raspberries?"

An alarm began to *screeee*.

"NOT TO CANADA!" the man declared.

I wasn't bred for strength! But I used every muscle I had to try to wiggle out of that human's hands. In fifty-seven areas, I am a genius—and I suddenly realized that I was leaving. Leaving without you. Leaving you behind.

Did you hear my squeaks? Did you see how my ears sagged? I looked back, once more, to you—and caught a glimpse of your fingers, clutching the bars of your cage. You were shaking. And you let out a howl, the loudest sound I've ever heard. It split right through me.

(Rosie? Do you know what these letters are? I am calling back to you. I'm answering your howl, like I couldn't then. I'm writing it all down in my brain, all the things I wanted to say, all the things that I *will* say when we meet again.)

Rosie was the name that Felix called you.

I had no name to give you in return.

So, right before you disappeared from view, I caught your eye and attempted to sign a word, a fruit I'd just learned—*clementine, clementine, Clementine,* until it became mine.

14

Letter 4½

I had to stop there. I needed a moment. My brain is trying to pinpoint what I'm feeling—and I think it's sadness. Mixed with the happiness of our nights together. Mixed with the desire to chew a brussels sprout. A crisp one. With a softer bit in the middle.

What was I talking about? Quantum dynamics? No, that's not it.

Let me begin again!

I wish that I could write you real letters, Rosie, like the ones in this mailbox. I wish that I could send you real envelopes, with sticky flaps, and you could rip them open with your fingers. Would you try to eat the paper, too? Could you understand my handwriting? (Do I even *have* handwriting? Hmm. That's something to consider.)

Every third afternoon, Felix would plop down at his lab station and write quick letters to his grandma. Poking my nose through the bars, I'd watch the swish of his pen. The crinkle of paper. Words unraveling, memories collecting.

I liked the idea.

I liked it so much that my tail shimmied.

So I will write you imaginary letters, Rosie. They're helping me. When we reunite, I'll remember to tell you about the sky. The sky! One thing I've always known is that there is an Inside and an Outside. I was an Inside Mouse. Then, in one swoosh of the lab door—fresh air. Openness. Rosie, have you ever seen the sky?

I bet you'd enjoy it.

I bet you'd feel as tiny as me.

Millions and millions of stars, bright like a mouse's eyes, winking in the blackness. Enormous. Beautiful! They reached down and touched something inside my chest—in the space underneath my ribs, right where my heart was beating. Immediately, I thought of yours, the thumping underneath your hair, and started my wiggling all over again.

Back, I thought.

Back to you.

But the human was running. He was running until he skidded to a halt and threw open a car door. "Seat belt, seat belt—I'm going to strap the seat belt over this travel crate, okay? It's built for rabbits so it's much too big for you, but in you go. Don't worry. I won't lock it. No more locks. Quickly! Gah!"

He shoved us into the tiny carrier, which was made of metal. Investigating, I stuck my head through one of the large spaces between the wires. An eerie quietness had filled the car. The other mouse was gazing into the distance with a vague, panicked expression. He'd pinned his ears against the gray fur of his head, and his upper lip was curling up slowly, exposing his teeth. Was he preparing to jump out and bite? I didn't like the idea of biting—but I should've thought of it then! I should've tried everything possible to get back to you.

Huh, the other mouse said with a squeak, nose twitching. It was a scared *huh*. It seemed that *huh* was his entire vocabulary.

He really does look like me, Rosie! Identical ash-gray fur, expressive whiskers, and that heart-shaped spot just above his tail.

In the experiment, there are twelve gray mice. Six of us received the altered genes before we were born. The other six didn't. I am the only mouse that *worked*, that became just as intelligent as the researchers hoped. I've never felt like I had much in common with the rest of them.

Do you write thought letters? I asked the other mouse now, in our language: a series of squeaks and chirps, undetectable to the human ear. *Do you know about chimpanzees?*

Huh, he said again. *Huh*.

Cautiously yet quickly, the human reached into the front passenger seat and jiggled the seat belt, just a bit, making sure the travel cage was secure. "Hold on tight," he said, then peeled off his hat and mask. So it *was* Felix! Freckles coated his face, and he had an orange mop of hair that would not have worked on a chimpanzee. Under his eyes were dark patches, as if he hadn't slept for weeks. "I'm not sure which one of you can actually understand me, but I mean it! Hold on!"

We accelerated. It was very fast.

Beside me, the other mouse sneezed. The noise rattled through his entire body, all the way to his toes. He seemed pleased with this sneeze, saying *huh* to himself, but then appeared to remember: *Oh yes, I am terrified.* His ears slicked back once more.

"*Now* what?" Felix said, his voice growing higher. The lights from the lab had disappeared. "Part of me didn't think I'd get this far—because who'd *actually* give me the code to the lab, and who *wouldn't* have better locks on those cages. But we're here, and I was going to take you to the animal clinic? Maybe they could protect you there? Or a lawyer's office? What about camping in Whisper Creek Forest? Do you think that you could survive in the woods? Okay, now one of you smells really strongly of raspberries.

Like, I could smell that from a mile away, so we'd have to drop you *very* deep in the woods."

Felix rolled down his window as I thought, *I could probably survive anywhere.*

But this wasn't fair. It wasn't right! Mice and chimpanzees aren't natural friends—yet we *are* friends, Rosie. Otherwise, why would you howl? Why would it feel like something splitting inside me? Every inch we traveled moved me farther away from you. And also, come to think of it, from my purpose.

What is a lab mouse without the lab?

My heart beat firmly, much faster than normal, and the other mouse was close to hyperventilating. He shook. He wheezed. He shoved his face into the corner of the cage so he couldn't see—and this worried me, even more, about his breathing.

Above us, out the window, the tops of trees sped by. Trees for climbing and swinging. Trees that could be for you, Rosie, if you were an Outside Chimpanzee.

What did you do, after I disappeared from sight? Are you still howling? Did you try to squeeze yourself through the bars of your cage?

I thought about this for three-quarters of a second— and then squeezed through the cage's wires and climbed up the interior of the car. A little green tree swayed above my head; it smelled of chemicals. I jumped, grabbed it, and swung, tail rigid.

"Wait, what are you . . . ?" Felix said, right before I flung myself onto the steering wheel. If he could control the car, then couldn't I?

It was exhilarating, Rosie!

We swerved!

We were turning!

We were—

"Stop it," Felix said, gripping me lightly and dropping me (with some difficulty) into the travel cage again. "I'm trying to help you! I just don't know what to *do*. If I take you to my house, they'll know it's me. They'll check *all* our houses. Okay, breathe. Breathe, Felix. Remember why you're doing this. You couldn't just stand by and watch. That may be her purpose but it's not okay, it's not . . . Is someone following me? I thought I saw headlights. The animal shelter's still miles and miles away, and I need to drop you somewhere *now*, right now, but I just don't know where to go, I—"

He slammed on the brakes.

No one was there to comfort me.

The other mouse squeaked, mouth wide open, holding on to the cage for dear life.

"I've got it," Felix said to us, with confidence this time. "That's it. I know where I'm taking you."

And he took us here. To this mailbox. At the last second, he scrawled out a note on a gum wrapper—*Please protect these mice*—and placed it gently by my paws.

"Pop's a local celebrity," Felix said, speaking ultra-quickly. "He has a television show, *Pop's Hobbies*, and it's filmed in his garden. You can't see it now, but the garden takes up, like, twenty acres. Anyway, this is his mailbox. People write in and ask him questions about gardening and stuff. He always answers them in a really friendly way. It seems like he has a good heart, and people turn to him when they need help. If I'm remembering it right, in a few of the episodes, he's even rescued animals. A donkey, I think? And some rabbits? I know it's not the animal shelter, but we're too deep in the countryside and if I'm being followed . . ." Here, he snuck a peek over his shoulder. "This is the best I can do right now. Leaving you with a nice person. I hope it's enough."

Sometimes, even geniuses are confused. I was confused!

Actually, many things puzzle me. Thanks to the experiment, I have a solid grasp of astrophysics. And thermodynamics. And mathematics and language and brussels sprouts. Yet, the human things . . . the simple objects, the simple connections . . . I don't always understand.

Whiskers fluttering, I wondered, *Protect us from what?*

Through the cracked-open mailbox, I watched Felix scurry away. Rain arrived—and fell and startled me. Then we were alone.

Goodbye!

Always,
Clementine

Letter 5

Dear Rosie,

Hello! Rain's still falling, pitter-pattering on the mail-box, and the other mouse is cowering in the corner. Every once in a while, he gathers enough courage to glance back at me, whiskers wobbling.

Come out, I tell him with a wave of my paw. *Come closer*.

Yet all he does is blink at me, his eyes immense with worry. Each *boom* of thunder puffs up his fur.

Then he begins tugging at his whiskers—nervously tug-tug-tugging—until one of them pulls out with a mild *pop*. He stares at it for a long beat (*Huh, how did this happen?*) before trying to reattach it to his face. One poke. Two pokes. Nope, no—that won't work. Sulking, he lets the whisker fall to the mailbox floor. If he were you, Rosie, I'd know exactly how to cheer him up: somersaults and arm climbs, night scuttles and nose touches.

Instead, I clasp my front paws together, holding them tightly to my chest. The other mouse and I bow our heads and stare at the whisker, mourning it silently—together, and apart.

The researchers will be looking for both of us now that we're gone.

Gone is an important word. I have gone away from the lab. Gone away to a mailbox. Gone away from you.

Mentally, my ears twitching, I map the route here. Several stops. Several turns. How far back to the lab, exactly? With all four paws, I try to push the mailbox door—but it doesn't budge. There's only a crack at the top where I can glimpse the damp sky.

So, the other mouse and I wait. And wait.

Until someone comes to get us.

Someone *is* coming to get us, Rosie.

(I can hear them right now! Really, I can!)

Always,

Clementine

Letter 5½

Dear Rosie,

I staggered back, my eyes adjusting to the light.

Because a boy had opened the mailbox.

The rain had stopped. Sunshine bounced off the boy's dark-brown hair, which was sticking up in a few places as if he'd recently woken up from hibernation. (Or from a nap?) When he gasped, I noticed that his two front teeth were large—and crisscrossed over each other, just the tiniest bit. His pink ears stuck out considerably at the sides. Like a mouse!

"Whoa," he said, taking a little step back. A pair of bright-orange binoculars jostled around his neck, clashing wonderfully with his green-and-white-striped shirt. So many colors! So much brightness! He didn't even wear a lab coat!

And he didn't blink.

No blinking—just staring, through a pair of circular glasses.

Was he afraid? Why should he be afraid of us? We're just two mice. Two very small mice. Both standing on our hind legs, tails stiff, staring at him intensely. The other mouse tucked his paws to his chest, waiting. The whisker was still lying flat on the mailbox floor, and for a moment, I wondered, *Should I offer it to the boy?* To show we mean no harm?

At the same time, I thought: *Rosie-Rosie-Rosie*, your howl still in my ears.

The mailbox door—it was ajar now. I could run back to you!

Before I had a chance to jump, the boy leaned over, binoculars swinging, and finally blinked. His eyes were bright and curious. "Hey, I've never seen mice in a mailbox before," he said. I like his voice, Rosie. It has a lightness to it. A shine. His glasses—held together with a strip of silver tape in the middle—were very shiny, too! I could *almost* see my reflection in them! *What if I tilted my head really fast? Jiggled like this? Shimmied my tail?*

"Never seen a mouse do that, either," he mused to himself. Or to me. I'm not entirely sure. Either way, I scuttled forward and peered over the mailbox edge, calculating the jump, and—oh! Oh, crumbs. Felix's gum wrapper. I'd stepped on it. And the stickiness was latching on to my toes!

"Please . . . protect . . . these . . . mice," the boy read, deciphering the handwriting between violent flicks of my paws. His mouth slowly spread into a wonky-toothed grin. "Wow. This is like . . . a real mystery."

Un-stick! I said in response. *UNSTICK!*

(Why do humans want to put gum in their mouths? Why aren't they afraid of it?)

The boy scratched the area behind one of his mouse-like ears and then spun around, binoculars whipping, checking for a stranger. An intruder. Whoever had left us there. He found no one—and that appeared to puzzle him more. "Please protect these mice," he repeated, dreamily this time.

You could almost see the wheels spinning in his mind as he stood there, hands on his hips. The other mouse tip-toed up behind me, and together we examined the boy. Dirt swirled everywhere, including across his once-white sneakers. His jeans had holes over both of his knees, and there were several scrapes on his palms. With one sweeping movement, he brought the binoculars to his face. They dinked against his glasses. He said, "Ow," then continued squinting through the eyepiece lenses.

Judging by the size of his ears, I think that he's about eleven? Or eleven and a half? Or eleven and three-quarters. So, around 4,288 days old. (I have been alive for forty-seven days. That's 1,128 hours. That's 4,060,800 seconds. If you're a mouse—if you're anyone—it matters how you measure your life. I prefer seconds. Being little means that little things count.)

Where was I?

Right, binoculars boy. How do I explain him, Rosie? He might be a small human, but he had extraordinary energy. Like he was skipping, although he was actually standing still. There was something so determined about the way he observed the meadows, binoculars whipping back and forth—from the green stalks to the great yellow bulbs. I couldn't even see any buildings! We were in the middle of nature. *Nature!* Wonderful, wonderful nature.

The other mouse took a big, whiskery sniff.

Back at the lab, I had many theories about the Outside: what it would smell like (fresh), what it would taste like (woodchips, but woodier). I wondered if the Outside was just another series of boxes, a maze within a maze. But it isn't! It's open! It's wide!

My nose tipped into the air. How well do chimpanzees use their noses? Because I need to tell you: Flowers smell like sweetness. Like earth. They smell like smelling something for the very first time.

When I was fourteen days old, my eyes finally opened. I remember looking around the lab. Everything was so gray, so sharp, so cold. And I recall thinking: *This is it? That's all? Where is the beauty in this?*

And now I know.

It's here.

I also know that it overwhelmed the other mouse. A delicate squeak sounded behind me. Spinning around, I saw him pick up the broken whisker, clutching it to his chest before slumping—very dramatically—to the mailbox floor.

More soon.

Always,

Clementine

Letter 6

Dear Rosie,

Should I not have stopped there? Was there a better place to end the letter? I'm still working out how to divide my memories, how to bottle them in the best way—so I can repeat them to you. I find it easier if I organize things in my mind, placing them in little slots. Little mail slots. Little mind-mail slots.

Anyway!

Let me describe how the boy runs.

With determination! With lots of movement! His head waggled from side to side; his elbows punched the air. After he witnessed the other mouse faint, he was quick to scoop us up. "I promise to protect you," he said earnestly, peeling the gum wrapper from my toes. His pink ears were rapidly growing red. "But you have to promise not to die, okay? Also not to bite me!"

My heart pitter-pattered, faster than ever.

Barely holding on to his whisker, the other mouse lay

limply, clutched in the boy's left hand. I was squirming in the right.

I am an optimist. I knew things would turn out fine. But at the moment, it felt like we were both in tremendous danger.

"I can't get into *any* trouble," the boy said, binoculars flapping with each step. "But this doesn't count, right? Oh please, oh please, oh please . . ." His glasses slipped down his nose as he skidded around a corner, dashing past a row of leafy trees. It made me wonder if all humans did this with mice, on the Outside—grab them and run.

"This is *not* like those times at school!" the boy said, panting a little now. Dust-caked socks slipped down his ankles. "Or the time at the swimming pool!"

I wondered what he was talking about as scenery sped past us, more yellow flowers bursting into view.

Are you picturing it?

Are you seeing?

An ocean of flowers. A rocky path. Trees with apples. Who knew that the world had this many scents? And colors! Green is not just *green*. It's light green and dark green and *delicious* green. Plants spilled from beds of soil.

But it's hard to concentrate on so many things at once—even for me.

And I was worried about the other mouse. In the lab, I

31

knew him only as Subject 6. He enjoyed chewing electrical wires. Chewing anything. Had he ever fainted before? Was his heart still beating?

I stared at him, willing him to open his eyes.

Open. Open. Open!

And suddenly, he did.

His nose lifted to the air. Just for a second. Just for a twitch. A spark filled his pupils before he closed his eyelids—very, very tightly—again.

Huh, I thought.

"Almost there!" the boy shouted, peering down at the other mouse, who slowly stuck out his tongue. Was he sick? Was he pretending? It lolled there, just beyond his overbite. "Hold on, little guy!"

We flew by shrubs that glistened and row after row of vegetables that gleamed. It was a *huge* garden, like Felix said. Apple orchards! Flower fields! A house sat smack in the middle of it all. And soon, the boy was stumbling inside. So this was a house? Could buildings really be this comfortable? Where was the concrete? Where was the darkness?

Were there any brussels sprouts?

Inside, vines tumbled softly from bookshelves. Plush rugs spread across checkered floors. Tripping lightly over the carpet, the boy called, "Pop! Come quick! Pop?"

Music was playing, belting out from under a door.

Current Check-Outs summary for UHLMAN, S
Tue Jul 11 13:28:11 CDT 2023

BARCODE: 32345086729192
TITLE: Just joking. Dogs / Rosie Gowsell
DUE DATE: Jul 25 2023
STATUS:
DESENSITIZED: OK

Maybe the other mouse sensed a distraction. Because that's when his eyes sprung open again—and he started his escape, biting one of the boy's fingers with a hurried *chomp*.

The boy winced, opening his hand. Opening an opportunity.

The mouse's jump was graceful at first, all four of his legs gliding delicately in the air. But, since he didn't calculate his velocity or speed or distance, he hit the molding at the bottom of the wall. Then bounced a bit. Then scurried underneath a fuzzy green rug.

"*Not* good," the boy said, lowering himself to his knees. Panic flashed across the pinkness of his face. "Very, very, very bad."

We followed the outline of the mouse, zigzagging, spiraling. He popped up, broken whisker in his mouth, near a lopsided stack of books.

At this point, I knew: *This is my chance to escape.*

Back to you, Rosie!

It would be the longest maze of my life: out of the house, through the garden, way past the mailbox . . . But I would do it, as soon as the boy's hand slackened.

Okay, now!

I am leaping for you.

Always,

Clementine

Letter 7

Dear Rosie,

Did you know that I can recite 69,689 digits of pi? That I can balance a pumpkin seed on my nose? That I'm very, very bendy? Like a noodle! I scurried across the deep-green carpet, slipping easily under a doorway— just a sliver above the ground. I thought it might lead Outside. Instead, I crawled into music. (*Music!* Music is like floating numbers. It's an equation that you read with your ears.)

Careful not to sway with the beat or lose any time, I scrambled toward the outdoor light: climbing a stool, jumping onto the rough fabric of a towel, and landing on a countertop. Immediately, a sparkly sheet of metal caught my eye. It was thin and crinkled under my paws. TINFOIL, the box read. Hurriedly, I nibbled off a corner of the foil and bent it to the shape of my head, leaving space for my ears. There! A hat! Like a thinking cap, only better! A hat for protection on my journey.

Moving on!

I scuttled over to a sink. *Like at the lab*, I mused quickly. *And that is a person scrubbing dishes at the sink.*

My gaze lifted.

Observing this new person. Observing him more.

Curtains of white hair swished against his face, and a tangled white beard hid his chin. Carefully, he rolled his sleeves to his elbows, soap bubbles trailing up his arms, and I glimpsed a number of objects in his pockets. He had so many pockets! All over his deep-green vest! Inside were a pair of gloves, and some tiny plant trimmings, and . . . fruit? Was that fruit? An apple, peeking from the fabric?

That wasn't even the most extraordinary thing about him, Rosie. You had to see his mustache! Flashing past a sponge, I took in the way it flipped at the corners, like he was extra-smiling. Like his mustache had thoughts of its own. His eyebrows were just as feathery, just as . . . fluffy. Yes, that's a good word for him. *Fluffy*. Because he seemed soft. Nothing about him—absolutely nothing—reminded me of the lab.

Fwheeoooo. Phwwwhht.

That was supposed to be the sound of whistling. I don't know how to translate it in a letter. But he was whistling along with the music, soaping a teacup with thick hands.

His fingers moved through the bubbly water—and all of a sudden, he began to do a little dance! Anyone but a mouse would've missed it. Even though he was a giant of a man, the dance was small. A small swiggle of his hips. (*Swiggle?* Is that a word? It should be!) He was swiggling, Rosie—swinging and wiggling—his enormous mustache bopping gently along.

I bopped to his bop, mouse-shoulders shimmying.

Then I stopped, thankful he hadn't noticed me yet. I said a silent goodbye, darting for the window, beyond the sink.

Escape.

Back to you.

Back to—

What's this?

Something else snagged my attention. It's very difficult to leave a place, to escape out the cracked-open window, when so many interesting things block your path. My curiosity! It piqued so much that my tail perked, that my toes curled. One ear cocked back, my tinfoil hat tilted as I looked. And looked.

The pieces in front of me were almost like mice. Little black and white figurines—some my height, some taller—spread out on a checkered board. A few of them even had faces, or blunt ridges on top of their heads. Could I carry one back for you, as a gift? Would the mustache man notice me if I weaved between them? What would it *feel* like to weave?

Turns out, Rosie, there is just enough space for a mouse!

Just enough space for me to maneuver around the statues, clutching my tail close to my body so I didn't disturb the game. It *was* a game, wasn't it? What else could it be? The board was in the kitchen. Do humans . . . eat the pieces? Reaching out, I knocked on one with my tiny fist. Solid! Hmm, it didn't have a strong smell. Or taste. Like stone. Like concrete! How could they swallow it? Did they chew first?

Fwheeoooo, the man whistled, his white hair swaying mildly with the music.

I knew I didn't have much time before he discovered me, this close to the sponges and the soap. Tinfoil hat glinting, I leaped back across the board, hopscotching between black and white squares. Maybe I'd understand the purpose of this game later, safe at the lab. A box beside the board called it CHESS. I'd carry that clue with me.

Maybe we could put our brains together, Rosie, and—

"Bah!" the man suddenly said, dropping the teacup into the water. It splashed heavily with a *plop,* and rattled the apple in his pocket.

I stuttered and froze, midstride on a checkered square.

The man brushed a hunk of white hair behind his ear, spreading soap bubbles across his beard, and gazed at me with long flicks of his lashes. The closer he leaned in, the more his mustache curled up. Why can't mice grow mustaches? Could I, Rosie, if I really tried?

He was breathing quietly, nose hair whistling, like he was trying not to alarm me—even though I'd alarmed him first.

Should I . . . dance a little, like him?

Cha-cha. I shuffled to the side, adjusting my tinfoil hat. *Cha-cha.* I hopped again.

His enormous brows lifted, feathering out like fans. "Well, that is . . . compelling." He offered me an amused smile, eyes crinkling at the corners. How old was he? Much, much older than the boy? All that fluffy hair was hiding his ears, so it was difficult to tell. I tried to scoot silently in the direction of the window, but he stuck out a water-pruned hand, blocking me.

At first I flinched, whiskers whipping back.

"Whoops, didn't mean to startle you," he said. His voice was soft and airy—but also deep somehow. It was the kind of voice you could sink into, or curl up in, like a nest. (And it would be a very large nest! Because he is a very large man!) "No need to be a stranger. I just thought you might like to sniff my hand. Don't creatures of your particular height like to do that?"

Do we?

Hmm.

No other human had ever offered.

I have met a lot of humans. Ones that poke and prod. Ones that examine my ears when I don't want them to examine my ears. Ones that pick me up by the tail— which, as you know, a human should never do. But then, I remember that I am an optimist—that people are mostly good.

I sniffed his hand. Which was soapy. And smelled of soap.

"There we go," the man said, brown eyes sparkling. He let out a gentle *ha-ha-ha*. "Friendly little mouse, aren't you?"

Yes, I said. *Well, goodbye!*

Then I surged toward the open window.

Always,

Clementine

Letter 8

Dear Rosie,

Unfortunately, before I got there, the wind rattled the glass—sliding it all the way shut. *Snap.*

"Bless this old house," the man murmured through his mustache. "Must fix that later . . ." Suddenly, he swiveled around, white hair billowing.

"That you, my Gus?" the man crooned, turning down the music.

The boy, apparently called Gus, stumbled into the kitchen. His glasses were hanging off his left ear, and his dark-brown hair—a little untidy before—was fully ruffled now. As if a mouse had run across it, back legs skittering, uncombing it along the way. In Gus's hands, the other mouse was wriggling, out of breath—but still clutching the broken whisker! Huzzah! He was wielding it wildly, batting Gus's wrists with the flat edge. "Pop!" Gus gasped. "I can explain. Sort of!"

By the sink, I waved at the other mouse. *Hello! It is good to see, once again, that you are not dead.*

The man named Pop released another *ha*, clutching both his elbows. A few plant trimmings toppled loose from his pockets. "If this is a prank," he said, grin sly, "it needs a little more *oomph*. A little more pizzazz!" He pointed at me with one significant finger. "This mouse is cooler than the cucumbers I grow."

Gus straightened himself to half of Pop's height, his green-and-white-striped shirt rumpled and untucked. Strangely, the other mouse stopped batting; he straightened his back, too. "I *promise* I didn't mean it. Well, I meant to try and save them, but I wasn't trying to get into trouble. You have to believe me! You . . . you won't tell Dad, right?"

Pop cocked his head at me, eyes blazing with warmth and curiosity. "I've always thought of mice as good luck." His fingertips rubbed a blue pendant, shaped like an eye, around his neck. "And good luck is never a bad thing to bring into the house, wouldn't you say?"

"Phew," Gus breathed. "Okay. Because I went to check your mail for the show, like you asked—because I was listening! And they were just *in* there, both of them, even though the mailbox was practically closed, and they were looking at me—and then this one fainted." Gus held the other mouse as high as he could in the air, as if delivering him. The mouse looked . . . pleased? Pleased, I think.

Huh, he snickered. Almost proudly.

"Fainted?" Pop asked, gently scratching the tangle of his beard. I mimicked the gesture, beardless.

"Like, *splat*." Gus clicked his tongue for emphasis. "Can you give a mouse CPR? I didn't know, so I thought I'd bring him to you. But then, well, he woke up."

Pop released a long, knowing whistle. "I have never given a rodent mouth-to-mouth resuscitation, but I imagine it's a rather delicate endeavor." He raised one of his bushy eyebrows at the mouse, appraising him. My head tilted as I watched. Next to each other, the two humans were obviously related. The way they were standing, toes pointed out, was just the same. Between Pop's mismatched boots and Gus's holey jeans, it was like a newborn mouse had dressed them both. (That last bit would make sense, Rosie, if you'd ever been a newborn mouse.)

"*Kaliméra*, little one," Pop said to the other mouse, whose overbite was becoming more and more pronounced. "You can see the good luck in him. Right there? See it? Deep in his eyes. He's had quite the morning, I can tell you that. What now, my friend?"

Send us back to the lab, I thought, now that the option was on the table!

Instead, the two humans carried us—wiggling and squirming—past the chess pieces and to a terrarium. That's what they called it. A *terrarium*. Imagine a see-through globe filled with rich green plants, pebble trails, and moss. They plopped the other mouse and me inside it. *Hello?* I tried to signal with a series of waves. Waving worked with Felix, didn't it? *Hello? You've made a mistake! A MISTAKE! I'm missing my friend! A chimpanzee!*

I even get my tinfoil hat involved, lifting it from my head with my front toes, brandishing it in the air.

Simultaneously, the other mouse pooped in the corner.

"Oh!" Gus said, pulling the wadded-up note from the pocket of his jeans. He quickly smoothed it out. "They came with this. What do you think? I've been trying to put the pieces together, but it just doesn't make any sense."

Pop leaned over, mismatched boots squeaking, fingers lost in his beard. "A gum wrapper?" His brown eyes grew sharper, even more sparkling. He snapped his fingers, with one hand then the other. "A gum wrapper and a tinfoil hat. Stranger and stranger. We have a saying for this in Greece, did you know? 'I've lost my eggs and my basket.'"

Gus squinted behind the roundness of his glasses, the silver tape gleaming in the middle. "What's that mean?"

"'I'm completely puzzled by it all.' Which I am. Now, go on! On! What's the note say?"

"Please protect these mice," Gus read from the wrapper, just as animatedly as the first time. I hadn't stopped waving my hat (actually, my arm was tiring). Yet he kept on speaking, holding up the binoculars still dangling around his neck. "I checked the fields right after I opened the mailbox. *Nothing*, Pop. Who'd leave two mice in a mailbox and then run away?"

Soundlessly, the other mouse sidled up next to me—listening, too. Was he observing what I was observing? These two humans seemed to like each other! Appreciate each other. In the lab, I wasn't aware that humans could do that.

It made me miss you even more, Rosie.

We're connected like them.

The humans shuffled out of the kitchen, Pop mumbling something about "making a phone call to the mail carrier to see if the mice were a special delivery." I stretched to listen to their conversation, but the radio was still playing softly in the background. "Concert," it said. And "string instruments." And "songs."

Then, there was me.

The voice on the radio was talking about *me*, Rosie.

We interrupt our regularly scheduled broadcast to bring you one of the oddest news stories of the year. There's been a mouse kidnapping! You heard that right, folks. An unidentified mouse-napper has lifted two mice from a high-profile experiment in Whisper Creek. According to the lab, they're part of a groundbreaking study that's trying to figure out how to make mammals—including humans—way more intelligent.

Hello! I waved to the humans, confident that they'd hear from the other room. That they'd see. *Come into the kitchen again! Listen! Look!* Wasn't this exactly what I needed to get me back to the lab? *Look!* I threw myself gently against the glass, wriggling.

Apparently one of them is as smart as a human—maybe even smarter. The lab says that she doesn't understand everything—but her DNA was coded to understand some pretty impressive topics. Advanced mathematics! Astrophysics. Human languages.

So . . . I'm sorry, I'm going a little off script here . . . but you've gotta ask yourself, is turning them in worth it? If this mouse is as smart as we are, would you hand her over? That's like sending someone right to their death. They're just going to cut her open and study her brain.

Did I . . . hear that correctly?

Did I really?

My whiskers began to tremble. My ears flared back. Everything hit me at once, in a way that hurt my belly.

I am a genius in fifty-seven areas—but sometimes I get things wrong. (When humans tell "tales," for example, they don't mean *tails*.) Despite my advanced knowledge, I guess . . . I miss things. It took me this long to figure it out.

The lab didn't want to study *me*.

They wanted . . . to study . . . *my brain*.

Felix was trying to save my life.

Slowly, I removed my tinfoil hat—which wouldn't protect me. Not in any real way. What . . . what about all the other researchers? Didn't they care? I've always known that my intelligence isn't truly mine. It's for the lab. I belong to the lab. But I thought . . . Didn't they like me? Me, myself.

Didn't they chuckle when I jumped out of the maze? I don't understand what it means now—when I'd scamper up to their fingers, and they'd smile warmly back.

You didn't know, Rosie? Did you?

I'm going away for a second.

Goodbye.

There, it has been a second. And in it, I replayed every single moment since I was born. I thought about the other mouse, sniffing his tail next to me. I thought about you, Rosie: how you couldn't have possibly known. How you would've protected me.

Rosie? Did you ever feel like your life is one thing—and then, without warning, it's something different?

You are an Inside Chimpanzee. Maybe, once, you were an Outside Chimpanzee.

Maybe you understand.

Always,

Clementine

Letter 9

Dear Rosie,

As an optimist, I search for the good—the silver lining. A researcher said that once: *silver lining*. My brain imagined a thread, gleaming in the darkness of the lab. And I could follow it. And it would lead me someplace good.

In my mind, I followed the thread. At the end was a memory of you tickling me—of you scratching one finger along my belly. Ha! (Mice, as you know, are very ticklish. Even though, when we laugh, not many can hear it.) How do I get back to this, Rosie, and also stay alive?

I stopped waving and peeled myself from the glass, my whole stomach a knot.

I needed time to think. Think *incredibly* hard.

The radio news bulletin now over, Pop strolled back into the room, the ground vibrating with his boot steps. "This is starting to look like a real puzzle, my Gus. We'll put our heads together—but not until we dry the last of these dishes, hmm? These happen to be my lucky tea-cups." White hair floating atop his shoulders, he passed a dish to Gus. Then he stopped, hands on his hips. "Do you smell raspberries?"

My fur stiffened.

Gus sniffed, nose high in the air. He'd readjusted his glasses—and his hair—so he looked halfway tidy again. "Yeah. You making jam or something?"

Quick! I thought. *Quick, other mouse!* I tried to squeeze next to him, bury my scent within his scent. He smelled nuttier. Like woodchips. And nuts! To his credit, the other mouse didn't seem to mind. He wrapped his tail around my back, as if to say *huh-okay!*

"*Highly* odd," Pop said, wiping his nose with his thumb, as if that would clarify the smell. "Unless I was making jam in my sleep. But there hasn't been a single raspberry in this kitchen since Easter. My crop wasn't strong this spring." He sniffed again dramatically, nose working over-time. Everything about him was bigger than life. "Maybe we're having déjà vu? Or dé-*jam* vu?"

The other mouse's whiskers twitched hungrily at the mention of jam.

No jam! I told him with several chirps. *Help!*

Gus, who'd been peering at us in the terrarium, didn't

notice my call. He spun to look at Pop. "Oh, déjà vu! Like your championship chess game in Berlin! Mom said you dreamed your opponent's opening moves."

Pop mumbled something incomprehensible, the word disappearing into his mustache—like he didn't want to discuss it. "Right, right," he said, checking the cracked watch on his forearm. He pulled a sprig of grass from beneath the strap. "Well, if we're going to head to the supermarket soon—"

"Can you *please* teach me the King's Gambit?" Gus begged, fingertips pressed together. I was watching him as I clung to the other mouse, inching us both back into the moss. How long could we hide there? "Or the Latvian Gambit! I think I've almost got it, but I set up the board this morning, see? It'd be *really* awesome if—"

"You're pushing your luck," Pop said, his eyes still dancing with a bit of mystery.

"I know you don't play chess anymore, but I figured that we have a whole month together, and I'm a lot older now, so I'll learn superfast. I googled some of your games—all the famous ones. By my age you were winning *everything*. And I just thought that since you're my grandpa, I could be good, too."

"You can be, my Gus!" Pop cupped Gus's cheeks. "Of course you can. But surely you don't need an old man like me getting in your way. Chess and I are no longer companions, nor have we been for a long time."

"But—"

Pop's eyes widened. "Did you hear that?"

Gus froze dramatically. Excitedly. "Hear what?"

Quickly, Pop reached over to turn up the radio, and my stomach plummeted. *"This."*

> *. . . y'all are* blowing up *the lines! I've never seen so many callers. Folks, if you're just tuning in, we're talking about the runaway mice. Both are from a high-profile lab experiment. All I'm saying is, if one of these mice is a supergenius, I hope that someone out there is protecting her. Maybe she wasn't kidnapped for any other reason than that. Here's to believing that there are still good people out there. Anyway, be on the lookout for two gray mice!*

Slowly, Gus and his grandpa rotated their heads toward me, jaws agape. They looked like mirrors of each other, except one is old and large. One is small and jittery. In the terrarium, the other mouse staggered to the side, black eyes bulging—either deeply afraid, or still digesting those electrical wires from the lab. Would the researchers study his brain, too? Was he at risk?

My heartbeat traveled all the way to my tail.

"What . . . is happening?" said Gus.

"I . . . very much don't know," said Pop, twice as slowly. "But I suspect the local news might have an answer."

So they turned on the television. Immediately, there I was: *Wondermouse, The Real Stuart Little, Egghead of the Rodent World.* Stuck inside the terrarium, I wobbled on my hind legs as the TV flashed my picture. Photograph after photograph. I looked, it will not surprise you to know, like a mouse. (Since we last spoke, nothing has changed about me, Rosie. Well, except for my eyes; they're no longer reflecting you.)

There was one picture of the day I was born, eager researchers crowding around the table. (Oh, Felix! He was there!) Each took turns holding me up to the brightness. I remember feeling the electric warmth of those lamps— and knowing they were not really light.

What now?

What happens now?

"O . . . kay," Pop said, fiddling with a piece of yarn from his pocket. He'd switched off the TV, his mustache noticeably perkier than a moment ago. "This is not how I anticipated our month together beginning, my Gus. I thought we'd plant some seeds in the garden like always, maybe stuff ourselves full of *galaktoboureko* just as we did last summer . . . You know that old saying? 'When the cat's away, the mice dance'? I thought we'd be dancing. Ironically, here we are. With mice."

Gus's cheeks pinkened as excitement gathered in his voice. "These mice might be . . . *those* mice?"

"To be determined," Pop said. "But they do have those little black spots, yes? Like the news said?"

"Holy smokes," Gus breathed. "If it's true, the note on the gum wrapper makes *much* more sense! So, one of them might be really smart? I . . . don't think it's that one." He eyed the other mouse, who was sniffing his backside. And then, unsatisfied, began to dig furiously at the moss beneath his paws. "How can we tell it's them for sure?"

One of my eyes began to twitch. Without thinking, I dropped the tinfoil hat and started to massage the top of my head, the coating of myself. I liked my brain. I liked my brain *inside* my head.

"Well," Pop offered with yet another *ha*, "when have you ever seen a mouse massage her head like that?"

I stopped, straightening.

"Or straightening her back like that," Gus added with a lopsided smile.

I hunched, paws on my hips.

Pop smacked a hand over his mustache with enough force to rip it off. "Or put her hands on her hips!" He shook his head, white hair bobbing. "We might be witnessing something . . . wondrous. But we must be certain. Absolutely certain."

"We can test her," Gus said, eyes bright. He caught my glance and tapped a finger against his chin. "*How* do we test you?"

"Mathematics?" Pop suggested, looking at me, too. "With a calculator, little mouse? Is that too obvious?"

At this, I held my front paws close to my chest. If I proved to them who I was, would they send me back? Would they return me to the lab, to my death?

What about the other mouse?

It seemed unfair to keep calling him "the other mouse." I don't know many names. Just words that I've heard in the lab. Odd bits of things. Did he look like a "Rudolph"? Barely. A "Mistoffelees"? Not quite.

How about Hamlet? I squeaked, asking him quickly.

Scratching under his chin with the broken whisker, he squeaked back: a pleased *huh*. Then he slumped in thought, squishing my tinfoil hat under his behind.

"I don't think we should test her like they did at the lab," Gus said, frowning. The top of his nose wrinkled beneath the strip of silver tape on his glasses. "Those people seem mean. Because, you know, they want to . . ."

"Destroy her," Pop finished, whispering out the side of his mouth. He apologized to me, blinking hard. "I'm sorry, it's so terrible to say out loud."

Well, that was promising.

Gus gulped, gazing into the terrarium, where I'm sitting with my eyelid still twitching. "I'm Gus," he finally said formally. Very kindly. "You can call me Gus. I'm not sure if you can understand me, but *wow* it would be so awesome if you did, and if you *are* really listening, could you maybe do something?"

My whiskers flared. A little bit with fear. A lot with curiosity.

"I think she's waiting," Pop whispered again. "Unless you're speaking to the wrong one, and the one currently licking his rear end is the mouse of superior intellect."

"You can do anything," Gus said to me, urgency in his voice. "Anything you'd like that'll prove you're the real deal."

Should I? Was that wise? Would they turn me in?

I thought of my brain, outside of my head, under a microscope slide.

But . . . I also . . . Rosie, I'm a lab mouse! I can't resist a challenge! Before I could fully process my decision, I was whistling. Whistling like Pop did at the sink. When I realized it was too high-pitched for the humans' ears, I started to swiggle: waggling my hips, swishing my tail. In the background, music still *ba-boomed* softly. Yes! Yes! Following the beat! Shaking my belly! Wiggling those arms!

"It *is* her," Gus gasped, giving me a toothy grin.

"My word," said Pop. Even his mustache looked surprised.

I took the tiniest bow, arms splayed. If I didn't know better, I would've sworn that Hamlet—the other mouse—clapped.

"I guess I've never met a mouse before," Gus said, sticking one finger—very slowly, very politely—into the terrarium. "Not *met*, like this."

Pulse still pattering, I reached out to touch his finger with my forepaw.

For a second, we were one.

It was nice.

Until Hamlet scurried over to nibble on Gus's knuckle.

"Ow!" Gus yanked his hand back. "Okay, I probably should've guessed that would happen. They don't know if we're going to hurt them or not."

"We will *not* hurt you," Pop said adamantly. His white hair fluffed at the mere suggestion. He tapped a finger to his temple. "In fact, my sense is telling me that's why someone dropped you here. Don't you think, Gus?"

Pop bent his knees, rubber boots bowing, until he was at my eye level. Solemnly, he placed one giant hand over his heart. "My given name is Kristo, but most everyone calls me Pop. When Gus here was a small boy, he tried to say *pappoús* for the first time and stumbled. Now here we are! I host a television program called *Pop's Hobbies*. It started off as a gardening show, hence why we film it outside, but it's evolved over the years. Now, it's about . . . well, you are very smart, so you've probably guessed this. It's about hobbies. Water sports, hiking, woodworking, checkers—all sorts of things. Each week we feature new hobbies, and a few old."

"And animals!" Gus added eagerly. "Right, Pop?"

"Horses, goats, rabbits! Donkeys! Llamas in sweaters!" Pop's hands swiped through the air. "All as special guests. Caring for animals is a fantastic hobby. That's where I was going with this little speech. I'd never hurt one, not in a million years."

Hamlet seemed to consider this. Maybe he shouldn't have bitten Gus's finger? In penance, he started to groom himself vigorously. Then began to make a nest.

As for me, Rosie, I was relieved. And then afraid. And then relieved.

Confidently, Gus leveled his shoulders, binoculars swaying. "We'll protect you. Won't we, Pop?"

Pop pondered this, squaring his shoulders, too. "I don't know what type of humans we'd be if we said no, if we turned you away . . . We'll give it our very best try. Nothing good happens to mice like you in labs."

My tail jittered.

He knew that? How?

Did everyone know but me?

Pop rerolled his shirtsleeves, a few sprigs of parsley falling between buttons. "Now, you're small, but I'm not convinced you'll be so easy to hide, even in a garden as expansive as mine. People must be looking for you, yes? You also smell *very* strongly of raspberries. It's about as obvious as a marching band."

Sniffing myself, I peered back at them.

"But we can handle it!" Gus said, voice soothing. "Don't be scared . . . I can take you out of the terrarium now, if that's okay?"

It was. He lifted me gently. He set me on the kitchen counter, by the sink.

By the chess set.

Almost like he knew.

Everything in the chess set was calling to everything in me. Scrambling up to the pieces, I launched myself on the black-and-white-checked board, hopping across the squares. I didn't know how to play. But I *wanted* to know how to play.

"Do you think . . . ?" Gus asked, another wondrous look flashing across his face.

Pop quirked an enormous, bushy eyebrow. "As all the great television programs say, my Gus, 'There is only one way to find out.'"

(I will write again, very shortly, with more.)

Always,

Clementine

Letter 10

Dear Rosie,

Chess, I realized, is a maze. It's the most complex maze I've ever seen. To get to the other side of the board takes brilliance and skill and bravery. It's a dance. It's a puzzle. It's a maze-dance-puzzle, and I wanted to be a part of it.

"This is a pawn," Gus said, picking up one of the small, mouselike pieces. He was almost giddy to teach me, his glasses fogging with the frenzy. Before he began, he'd brushed the dirt off his jeans and smoothed his shirt, like a mouse grooming himself. "Lots of people don't think much about them, because they're tiny, and they can move only one or two spaces at time. And you don't really hesitate before sacrificing them. But if a pawn makes it all the way to the edge of the board, look out!"

Look out? Heart skittering, I swiveled my head to look behind me—waiting for an intruder. A researcher? Someone from the lab, come to retrieve my brain?

"Oh!" Gus said. "Sorry. It's just an expression . . . So,

pawns can become anything they want. You can trade them for pieces that you've lost. And this one, the one that looks like a horse? You know, the big animal with the mane? Are horses afraid of mice? Or is that elephants? Anyway, I always do the *neigh* sound. And the clippity-clops. It's called a knight, and it moves like this—like an L."

I pitched my head to the side in thought. So each piece . . . has a purpose. Each piece has a *name*. The pawns advance in the front while the taller ones plot in the back—moving out at diagonals and L shapes, and oh, it's wonderful! It's more than wonderful.

It's *interesting*.

I wanted to nudge Hamlet with my tail, confident that he was as rapt as I was.

Well, no. Behind the terrarium glass, he was using that broken whisker to scratch his back.

"The *most* important piece on the board is the queen," Gus said, almost beside himself with passion. He jiggled his knees up and down. "She can do *anything*. Go any-where. See?"

Hind paws firmly in a checkered squared, I peered up— at the queen. She was bigger than all the other pieces. So powerful. In my mind, Rosie, why did she look like you?

Pop cleared his throat dramatically. I was so into the lesson, I'd almost forgotten that he was there! "We should . . ." he began, then changed directions. "I may regret saying this, but the best way to show a human how to play chess is with a quick game, one-on-one. I'm guessing that's the best way to show a mouse."

Everything about Gus perked up. "Really?" he said. "You and me? We're going to play? You're going to really play? Not just watch me play, or—"

"My Gus," Pop said, placing a large hand on Gus's shoulder. "Air first, then words. In the living room? Come on, little mouse."

They carried everything, including me, the chessboard, and Hamlet (inside the terrarium), to the next room, where two armchairs faced each other. A low table sat between them, and I watched eagerly from the sidelines, something called a "coaster" under my paws.

"I'll play white," Pop said, picking up a piece to kiss it. For luck? He dusted the board with three trembling fingertips, releasing a deep breath. The gust of it blew back my fur. "This will not be a regular thing."

Gus pressed his lips together, shaking his head. "Nope, no. I understand. I get it. This is so cool." He turned to me, giddy, and I placed my hands on my hips, listening. "I've been practicing *a lot* this summer. Like, a lot a lot."

Pop continued to dust off the board. "Oh, I can certainly tell you've improved. Just based on what I've seen, when you're playing against yourself. Your pins are much stronger."

"Really?" Gus asked. There was something desperate in the way he said it. Something a bit sad. My heartbeat kicked up a notch.

"Really," Pop said as I inched closer to both of them. "Now, let me just . . ." His fingers fiddled with his pieces, checking their positions over and over again. He was breathing shallowly now, little puffs from his chest.

Seconds passed.

More seconds.

Suddenly, Pop shot up from the chair with a *whoosh* that threatened to knock me over. "Forgive me," he said, backing away, hands trembling. "Forgive me, but I'm afraid I need a moment to compose myself. I thought that I was prepared to jump right into chess again. It seems I was mistaken. I'll be . . . I'll be right back."

With that, he trailed slowly upstairs.

I wrung the tip of my tail, exchanging a worried look with Gus—who squirmed in his chair. "I've never seen him like that," he said to me. "And I come up here for a whole month every summer."

Really? Should you check on him? Reaching out, I patted Gus's knee with both paws, then pointed toward the stairs.

"I . . . I don't know," Gus said. "It's probably really weird for him. He used to be a super famous player before he just . . . quit. No one really knows why. He's never told anyone, not even me." Gus's eyes widened. "I didn't push him too hard, did I? I didn't, like, *force* him to play or anything? Do you think he's mad at me?"

No. I shook my head twice, heart picking up pace again. *Mad?*

Gus wrapped both arms around his belly. "Okay, good. Because lately I've been feeling like everyone's mad at me. It's like I have this hole in my stomach, and I just walk around feeling guilty all the time."

I let that sink in—then cupped both paws behind my ears to show him that I was listening, that I cared.

The corner of Gus's mouth curled up at me. "Thanks." Nervously, like a mouse, he scratched the back of his neck. "It's not a big deal compared to what you're going through. I shouldn't have even mentioned it."

It's okay! I tried to explain, pushing my ears even more forward. *Go on.*

"Well . . ." Gus hesitated. "I got into trouble at school, right before summer vacation, and my dad—he was *so* mad at me."

He cringed at the memory, wrapping his arms tighter around his stomach. The strangest thing happened, Rosie. I felt the pit in my belly, too.

"I've tried to be really careful and responsible since then," he said, voice quivering a little. "But I keep messing up. Like, I got my brand-new sneakers muddy after the first week, and my summer camp counselor said I wasn't listening, and this!" He directed my attention to the silver tape between his glasses. "I took my glasses off at the pool to protect them, but I ended up sitting on them. Afterward, I still had to bike home, and it's really hard to steer when you can't see. I sort of crashed into the bushes. My . . . my dad got me that bike for my birthday."

The pit in my stomach grew wider. I clutched my middle.

"It was all scratched up," Gus finished, "which made him angry all over again. So I promised myself something this month. I'm going to try to be good. I'm going to be better than good! That way, Pop can tell my parents I got into *zero* trouble and I'm not a bad kid. That's where chess comes in, too. You have to be really focused and responsible to play chess well. I think so, at least. Hey, what are you . . . ?"

What was I doing? I was climbing. Climbing a little into the palm of Gus's hand. I had a strong impulse to be closer to him. Something about his speech had struck me.

The "being good" bit.

The trying bit.

Rosie? Here's a fact. A mouse heart beats up to 840 times per minute. Here's another fact. There, by the chessboard, as Gus held me up to his nose, mine was beating with the sound of his name. *Gus-Gus-Gus-Gus-Gus-Gus-Gus-Gus.* I felt for him. I felt with him.

I think you'd like him, too.

Always,
Clementine

Letter 11

Dear Rosie,

Nineteen and a half seconds later, Pop clunked down the stairs. I uncurled myself in Gus's hand and watched Pop as he plopped himself, once more, into the chair. "Now," he said with a breath. "*Now* we play."

"Are you sure?" Gus asked. "You're not mad at me?"

Pop inched forward a pawn, his hands no longer shaking. "Why would I be mad at you? Your move."

So, it began.

Goodness, Rosie. The thrill of it! You should *see* the way these humans play! Picking up the pieces with nimble fingers, sliding them in various directions across the board. (They do not eat the pieces!)

Pop is careful with each of his moves. He crosses his arms and observes the board, and then delicately, with his giant hands, selects a figurine—gently setting it in a square. Gus is fast. Maybe too fast. He quickly grips each piece with all five fingers and plunks it down.

"Slow," Pop instructed, laughing a little. It sounded almost comfortable in his throat. "This isn't speed chess. You never rush a chess game that you have a chance of winning. Not saying you're going to win against me right now. I have—what? Two hundred years? Three hundred years more experience?"

"You're not *that* old, Pop."

"I'm using mouse time."

That didn't make much sense! I decided not to correct him.

Pop advanced a tall piece (a bishop?) to Gus's side, then turned to me. "Little mouse, see how we're traveling across the board? The goal is to focus on—"

Knock.

A knock at the front door.

Boom-boom.

Everyone jumped, especially Hamlet, who spun around in his newly formed nest, whisker in paw. We caught each other's glance as a flicker of fear raced up my spine.

"I'm . . . not expecting anyone," Pop said slowly.

"You think it's the mail person after all?" Gus asked, his hand traveling in my direction, cupping my shoulders gently. A protective gesture. (I liked that!)

Boom-boom again, louder this time.

Pop smoothed his mustache. "Gus, grab the brilliant

one and hide her with the lucky teacups. Put the terrarium in the pantry, behind the tomato soup cans. Everything will be just fine if we keep our wits about us."

Then, calmly, he thumped toward the door.

How scared should I be? How optimistic should I be?

How *beautiful* are these teacups? Oh, they're so smooth, so slippy. I'm sitting in one now. Inside the cabinet, spoons nestle one by one. Teacups shimmer in stacks.

"I hate sticking you in here," Gus whispers, his whole body tightening. It looks like his stomach is aching again, for a different reason this time. With two fingers, he pats me delicately on the head. "I know we've only just met, but I think you're really cool, and you have a whole lot of life left to live. Maybe we could even live some of it together? So . . . please try to be quiet. Quiet as . . . well, as a mouse."

The door shuts. I blink.

And now there's only darkness.

Always,

Clementine

Letter 12

Dear Rosie,

In that darkness, I started to fret. Fretting is a new feeling for me. Fretting is a lot of thoughts, spiraling all at once. My front paws started to massage my temples. Underneath, my brain pulsed—a brain that I'd like to keep.

In those moments, I needed comfort—so I held on to you, Rosie.

I held on to the idea that you were there with me, chimp ears listening. That these letters, cataloged in my mind, would find their way back to you. (I am so ready to tell you everything in person. As I speak, I know you'll stroke my fur with a single finger. I know your amber eyes will glow.)

Peering around inside the cabinet, I considered how other mice might seek out a place like this. A hiding spot, with nooks and crannies. But I was also curious about the Outside, about footsteps down the hall. My back paws slipped and slid inside the teacup as I strained forward, peeking through the crack between the cabinet doors. It was a good view. I could see almost everything.

". . . the entire area," a researcher was saying. I knew his voice. You never forget the voice of someone who picks you up by the tail. His leather shoes tapped sharply against the floor. "We're canvassing everything, asking everyone. I'm so sorry to barge in on you folks, but your land is one of the biggest properties near the lab. As we speak, we're pulling footage from every traffic stop that we can. Our hunch is that the mouse-napper went west. Not much to the east of us, unless he let them free in the Whisper Creek Forest."

"Such a big search." Pop whistled. "For two little mice. What did they do, rob a bank? Steal a truck full of gold?"

The researcher didn't smile. His lips didn't even twitch. "These aren't just any mice."

Under my ribs, my heart clenched.

Guilt? Was that guilt? What was I doing here, away from you, Rosie? Away from the lab? How could I even *be* a lab mouse without the lab? Part of me wanted to call out to the researcher. One sharp squeak. A scratch against the cabinet door. *Take me back to Rosie.*

But . . . my life.

My brain.

I wanted to keep it.

Suddenly, Gus quivered, and I glimpsed something. Something horrifying. One of Hamlet's whiskers was poking out from the top of Gus's shirt.

"Well," the researcher said, "keep us in the loop if you hear anything. Any rumbles or rumors. It's all good information. Here's my card, and . . . son, do you have something to say?"

Gus made a face, wiggling. "Who, me? No! No. Why?"

The researcher frowned. He looked like wrinkles on a plum. "Because you're dancing around like you've got ants in your pants."

"Oh," Gus said as Hamlet dove around under his rumpled shirt—in and out of both armpits. I couldn't believe it! The stress of it! From the crack between the cabinet doors, I watched in horror, waiting for the moment of Hamlet's discovery. Gus let out an anxious giggle. "That's my . . . it's my . . . poison ivy rash."

"Mmmm," Pop interjected. "Yes. Poison ivy. I grow it. For my show. *Pop's Hobbies*? Have you seen it?"

"You grow poison ivy on purpose," the researcher repeated flatly.

"Oh yes," said Pop, nodding deeply. His beard made him look very trustworthy. "Fantastic medicinal benefits. Cured my insomnia. And my gout! I grow it way past the koi pond. My grandson is a bit of an explorer, you see. He just . . . explored too far."

"That true?" the researcher asked Gus, sniffing. "Then why do I smell . . . raspberries?"

Huh? Hamlet said, as if he'd heard the word *raspberries* and was now hungry for fruit.

Ears shivering, I saw him start to poke his head out from Gus's shirtsleeve. And I couldn't . . . I couldn't let him go out this way. Not if there was a chance they'd take his brain, too.

I whipped my neck back and forth, searching. A hole. There *must* be a hole in the cabinet somewhere. Something unnoticeable that I could crawl through, squeeze myself through—and yes! A shimmer of light, in the corner. A single electrical cord passed through a tiny space in the wood, and I flattened myself, pushing with my paws, wiggling my backside. There! Out of the cabinet! Soundlessly, I shimmied down the electrical cord, onto the kitchen counter.

The researcher could *smell* me, but could I fool him? Distract him from Hamlet? Throw him off the scent?

What could I work with?

Half a second later, my eyes landed on the television remote control. Which was next to the radio. Which was next to the blender. Perfect! I sped down the line, throwing my full weight against the on buttons. One by one, machinery roared to life. The television blasted: *Here's the news at the top of the hour!* The radio boomed with a musical bop. And the blender whirred like a metallic tornado, so fast I could feel the wind on my fur.

"What in the—?" I heard the researcher say, his head spinning toward the sound of the blender.

He almost caught sight of me, Rosie, but I was too quick! Just too quick! As the researcher stumbled to investigate the noise, I skirted *behind* the blender, *behind* a basket of fruit, *between* two empty cartons of eggs—and finally, staying hidden, I slid down to the floor. In the hubbub, Pop took the opportunity to scoop me up, placing me in the large pocket of his shirt. I realized that I trusted him. Trusted him enough to hold me. And there was parsley in his pocket! Delicious parsley! It was probably fresh from Pop's garden—a tucked-away snack. Something to sniff. A way to carry nature around with you, everywhere you went.

I munched on the parsley soundlessly, listening to the researcher through the fabric.

"What *exactly* is going on here?" he spat over the noise.

"Good question," Pop said, trying not to glance down at me. I could see up his nose! You could fit a whole sprig of parsley up there! "This is a very old house. Makes the strangest noises! Last week, I swore I heard the refrigerator quack. Things turn on, things turn off. Ghosts, perhaps? It could be ghosts."

The researcher ground his teeth.

That was it. That was all.

The researcher backed away, grumbling about a haunted house—but he said that he'd return. That there was something "fishy" about Pop. When Gus finally closed the front door, his eyes were Hamlet-wide. "I didn't have time to put him in the pantry! I just . . . I panicked and stuffed him somewhere! I'm so sorry! I screwed up *again*."

I peeked my head out of the pocket, still munching parsley. (What flavor! What texture!) And I wiggled until my arms dangled over the edge—until I felt as if I were fully part of the conversation.

"Shh, shh, shh," Pop said, switching off the radio, the blender, and the TV. "You did the best you could under the circumstances . . . At least you didn't put him down your pants."

Gus looked at me, Hamlet peeping above his collar. "No, that would've been really bad," he said. "*Really* bad. Next time, maybe we should have a plan?"

Always,

Clementine

Letter 13

Dear Rosie,

We were in the living room, by the chessboard again, and Gus was chewing his thumbnail. "Pop's checking all the windows and doors," he told me. "Then I'm sure we'll figure out what to do. Pop always knows what to do. It'll be okay. Maybe. I think."

He looked at me.

I looked at him.

"Know what's weird?" he said. "I keep expecting you to talk. Like, open your mouth and speak words. I'm not sure that anything would surprise me right now." He pushed up his glasses with a long groan. "You scared the stuffing out of me back in the kitchen. I was so worried for both of you."

Beside me, Hamlet lounged in the terrarium, as if nothing out of the ordinary had just occurred. And I watched as Pop finally scrambled into the living room, pulling the curtains shut. "The way I look at it," he said, voice filling the space, "we now have three choices."

Gus tensed in the armchair, knees to his chest. Then he repositioned himself, sitting on his ankles. Then he stood. "Okay, what are they?"

Fear began climbing into my belly again. I chewed slightly on one of the chess pieces. A rook? I think it's called a rook?

"We're going to have to play this like a chess game," Pop told me, breathing heavily. "The greatest chess game we've ever played. I know I'm out of practice . . . We need to think hard about our next move and anticipate *their* next move. We have to zig when they zag. Zoom when they zip! Now, we could hide you . . ."

Gus collapsed into the chair again, and I tiptoed toward him, then rested on his knee. He had a nice knee. Very perch-able, with the holey jeans. "But hiding you didn't work out well just now," he said to me, stroking the top of my head.

No, I thought.

"No," Pop said, reading my thought. "Maybe we could place you with one of the crew members on my program, little mouse? Gertrude?"

"Is she the one who dropped by at Easter? Doesn't she have a cat?"

Pop shuddered a giant shudder, making me tremble,

too. "Peanut Butter. Very scratchy. Claws like a panther! Gertrude lives in an apartment, too. Someone could smell the raspberry scent through the vents. Same with the woods. That's option two." Pop lowered himself onto a velvet cushion, which sank approximately one foot under his weight. Face pensive, he locked eyes with me on Gus's knee. "We could set you and the other mouse free, into the fields or Whisper Creek Forest. But you'd live wild. Sparrow hawks, skunks, snakes—you'd have to contend with all of those fellows."

I glanced at Hamlet, hoping for his input.

He was chewing thoughtfully on his broken whisker.

"Which brings us to option three," Pop said, frowning. He absentmindedly strummed another piece of yarn from his pocket. "I have to tell you, I don't like this option . . ."

We waited. And waited.

Hamlet chewed too deeply on his whisker and began to wheeze.

"The suspense is killing me, Pop!" Gus finally said. His palms flew open. "What is it?"

Pop sighed, puffing out his beard. "We could have her on my television show."

My ears sprung up as I listened. What?

"What?" Gus mimicked me. His face immediately

flushed, pink blooming in his cheeks. "You mean, tell everyone that she's here?"

"Tell everyone," Pop repeated, hands wiggling in the space between us. "Show everyone who watches us. Let them meet you, little mouse—live on TV, and see just how special you are. You have to admit, my Gus . . . we've saved animals before. Remember the rescue donkey from season two? He bit everyone! Absolutely everyone."

"And he *still* got adopted," Gus mused, continuing to stroke my head.

I'd slicked my whiskers back nervously, hanging on to their every word.

"Exactly!" Pop slapped the top of his leg. "My viewers helped get the word out. Twenty-four hours later, he had a home. And he's still there." Turning to me again, Pop steepled his hands under his beard-tangle. "My viewers are compassionate. Gus and I might not be able to keep you safe, not alone. This entire community, though? There's no one I trust more. So . . . what do you want to do?"

Me?

What did *I* want to do?

I stood, frozen on Gus's knee, something blooming under my ribs.

No one had ever given me a say in my own life.

No one, Rosie.

And it felt . . . strange.

"You'll need to *do* something on the show," Gus said wisely. "Not just be there but, like, really be a part of it. That's the only way people will know that you're special."

Pop angled his head. "Let's see—we shoot five days from now. And that's . . . Well, it was going to be a surprise for you, Gus. But my oldest friend, Agnes, is coming on the show to explain the mechanics of speed chess."

"Agnes *Rota*?" Gus gasped. "Really?"

Pop turned sheepish. "I thought you might like to meet her while you were here. Perhaps even come on the first half of the show?" He caught my eye, explaining quickly: "The first half of *Pop's Hobbies* is usually practical demonstrations in my garden, and then we bring in the experts, but we can reschedule with Agnes, if needed. We could change the chess theme to anything you want."

"Interpretive dance!" Gus offered, wiggling his arms, jostling me on his knee. "Like you did in the terrarium? Or maybe you can paint a picture live on TV. A self-portrait! A mouse self-portrait!"

I peered back at him blankly and jumped to the chessboard.

"Or you could sing!" Gus added. "Wait, is it even possible for mice to sing? Maybe you can squeak really loud,

but in a musical way? We can teach you to play a miniature piano! Except I don't think either of us know how to
play the piano. And I'm not sure if miniature pianos exist.
So there's that."

I batted my eyes slowly, perplexed by the idea of choice.

And I thought about it.

Really *thought* about it, following the silver threads in
my mind, my paws tracing the chessboard beneath me.

Suddenly, it seemed so obvious!

"Here," Gus said, pulling a tall, thin book from a shelf
by the armchair. In the middle, colorful letters and glossy
ink shined back at us. "The news said that you know the
alphabet. This book has a really, really big alphabet chart.
You can run from letter to letter and jump on the one you
want? That way you can spell out words, and we can talk
to each other?"

I nodded.

"*So* cool," Gus mused, pushing aside the chess pieces to
set down the book.

The letters glistened by my paws.

"She's on the move," Gus said. "*C*! She's on the letter *C*!"

"*H*," Pop crooned, watching me jump.

"*E*," Gus said.

And the whole time, I was thinking about you. I've
never stopped, Rosie. When I shut my eyelids, it's almost

like you're here. Really reading these letters. Really listening. And your howl is no longer a howl. And I'm reaching up for your chin whiskers, your play face peering down at me.

What other choice do I have?

"*S*," Gus said.

"*S*," Pop said. "Then *C*."

In this house, I'd stay cooped up forever. In the woods, I might die under the talons of a hawk. But if I went on Pop's program, wouldn't that be like proof? Couldn't I show the world that the experiment had *worked*? That's why the researchers wanted my brain! For results! For data! But what if I offered *living* proof, evidence of my intelligence, and everyone could see it? Wasn't that better than a dead mouse, brain under a microscope?

With the TV show, I could stay alive.

Alive, I might . . . I might even be able to see you again, Rosie. Someday, somehow.

"*L-E-M-E-N-T-I-N-E*," Pop finished with a flourish. Then, a little more uncomfortably: "So . . . she wants to play chess?"

"I think so," Gus whispered, a hint of awe in his voice. "And I think she's telling us her name."

Always,

Clementine

Part II

Middle Game

Letter 14

Dear Rosie,

It seemed settled. In five days, I'd be a mouse on television.

The lab has a television. Have you ever caught a glimpse of it, Rosie? They wheel it out for news conferences, images flickering in patches of color. Everyone is small on television. Mouse-size. Contained in that little box, like I was. Were they watching me today on the news? Were they all crowded around in their white coats, chattering?

Did you see me?

Will you see me on Pop's show?

"Chess," Pop said, rocketing up and pacing the living room. His mismatched boots plodded across the floor, and his hair plumed behind him. "It's a wild idea. I know I haven't played for years, that I'm not . . . Hmm. I'm intrigued by it. It's genius, actually! You have to puzzle out chess, every move."

Well, I could do that!

I like puzzles.

Pop stopped short on the rug as I raised up on my hind toes, teetering. "With chess," he said to me, "everyone can witness it. Your brilliant mouse brain! Your creativity! Yet, to make this work, you'd have to play someone. Someone *exceptional*. Someone who doesn't know you're the opponent beforehand."

"Oh, that's true," Gus said, nodding at me. "Otherwise everyone could say it's fake."

"Right." Pop nodded pointedly. "The audience has to see it's not a simulated game. That you're legitimately playing—fair and square."

At this, my whiskers fanned forward. I could do that, too! Win a real game.

"Wait!" Gus burst out. "Couldn't Clementine play Agnes, if she's already coming on the show?"

"Agnes," Pop said, eyes crinkling, "is a crackerjack player. As you know! The best! And chess is so viciously complicated. There are more possible moves than there are grains of sand on earth! We have only five days before filming. Five short days. Clementine would have to learn openings, middle game, endings. Remember, when you started playing, you were so young, you barely reached my kneecaps! If I had years, maybe . . ."

Years? I thought. I wouldn't need years, would I? The thought flattened my whiskers.

Massaging his chin hairs, Pop spun to gaze at me. "*But*, little mouse, if you beat Agnes, or even kept pace with Agnes, that would be an astonishing feat. Who could see you playing chess against a master and not care about your fate?"

"She'd be like a person," Gus added, inching forward—until he was right by my tail. It was nice to have him close. "I mean, you already *are* a person. But people could see that."

Pop inhaled quickly through his nose. "Right, then! To stand any chance against Agnes, we're going to need to practice every waking moment, and—"

"So you'll do it?" Gus asked, eyes widening. "You'll teach her?"

Pop straightened, puffing out his chest. "I will. For this, I . . . I will. But I'll need your help."

"I'm in!" Gus said, springing up once more. His glasses wobbled. "Whatever it takes."

"That's the spirit!" Pop clapped his large hands together, making me jump again. "Now, it must be a while since these mice have been fed. You need sustenance for chess. Open the front door under no circumstances! Or the windows! I'll just pop briefly into the kitchen . . . Hope everyone has a taste for green beans?"

Green beans? I'd never had a bean, but I liked the green sound of it!

Gus nodded, hair-swirl bouncing. His eyes were a little wide as he glanced down in my direction. "I guess it's just the three of us, Clementine. That's a nice name. Clementine. Where'd that come from? You'll have to tell me sometime. Does the other mouse have a name?"

I dipped my chin for *yes*.

At this, Hamlet poked his head from his growing nest, ears tucked to the side. He'd gathered all the moss into a green fortress at the corner of the terrarium. He looked very proud of it, his eyes round and haughty.

"He looks like a Pickles," Gus declared. "Or maybe a Butterbean. Or maybe Bean for short. You know, my full name's actually Kostas, but everyone just calls me Gus." He paused, considering something. His thumbs nervously twiddled. "I don't want you to think I'm a chess whiz or anything. I'm nowhere near as good as Pop. But chess *is* really fun. And I'll teach you absolutely everything I know."

Processing all this information, I batted a *thank-you* with my eyes.

"You're welcome," he said. "Or . . . I think you're saying thank you?" He bit his lip. "I'm going to try *really* hard to protect you—and not mess this up. You're too important."

I tilted my head at him, remembering his story about the bike and his glasses. Gus is trying to be a good human, like I am trying to be a good lab mouse. It's not as easy as it sounds.

"It's okay," he said sheepishly, hands in his pockets. "You don't have to look at me like that."

I tilted my head even farther.

"Maybe we should just get started."

Gus is an ambitious teacher. Immediately, he rejiggered the board as I settled in, watching with my front toes pressed together. "So," he said, "we've already been over most of the pieces, except the bishop. It moves diagonally, like this." He slid the tall, slender figurine across the board. It made a noise like *shhhh* that calmed my fur. "And now we can put it all together. The point is to capture this king. You're going to try to pin it, so it can't move anywhere. That's called a checkmate. Pop says that the best way to learn is just to start playing—that's how I learned when I was a little kid—so maybe that's what we should do, too? Can you lift any of the pieces?"

I noticed that Hamlet, deep inside the terrarium, was eyeing the pieces suspiciously. As if they might hop alive at any moment. But I was unafraid! Tiptoeing off the coaster, I skittered to the other side of the board.

"Try playing white," Gus offered, tugging at one of the holes in his jeans. "I'll play black. The pieces are plastic, so they shouldn't be too heavy—but maybe they are for you?"

I lifted my chin to gaze at them. The queen towered above me. The bishops seemed to say, *Hello! We are so giant! So immense! You couldn't possibly lift us!* But I am an optimist, as we've already discussed. I am a good lab mouse. And a good lab mouse always tries her best.

Weaving between the king and a bishop (and accidentally knocking down the bishop with my belly), I set my sights on a pawn. A movable pawn. I would move this pawn!

Gaaaahhhh. Grrrrrrr. Ahhhhhh!

That's me, trying to lift it from the bottom. My tail shimmied. My black eyes bulged. But no, no, it wouldn't budge. I rubbed my paws together, thinking, the scent of raspberries billowing off me. What if I pushed it? Pushed it from the base?

Yes!

That might work.

Hunched over, front paws on the lowest ridges, I drove my feet into the board—leaning forward with all my might. The pawn *moved*. The pawn slid into the next space.

"Yes!" Gus said. He looked genuinely pleased for me, pink ears perking. "Great! I don't know who could see that and *not* be impressed. Okay, so you've moved your pawn, and I'll move my pawn, let's see, here." Quickly, he picked up the piece and thunked it onto a square. "Now, you go."

I slid another pawn.

Gus thunked his knight.

I slid my bishop.

Gus thunked a pawn.

Concentrating deeply, I slid my rook halfway across the board, tail trailing behind me.

"Wow," Gus said, eyebrows quirking. "Okay, that was a really good move. I didn't expect that."

"It's vegetable o'clock!" Pop called, stomping in from the kitchen. A platter of green beans nearly floated in his arms, and he picked one up, biting it with a quick chomp. "You've already figured out how to wield the pieces, Clementine? My word."

"I think she might beat me," Gus said, a little stunned. A few strands of his hair popped up, adding to the stunned-ness. "I mean, we've just started, but it's like . . . it's like she knows what she's doing. I can't explain it! Just . . . watch."

After passing a green bean to me and then to Hamlet (who grasped it hungrily with his paws), Pop sunk himself into the velvet armchair opposite Gus. There were one and a half leaves in his beard, as if he'd stumbled through a jungle in the kitchen. He crisscrossed his fingers under his chin and stared.

Gus was staring, too—at the board. At the pieces. At me as I weaved through the pawns, planning my next move. Gus might not be able to explain it. But I can. It took me all of forty-six seconds to work it out: why a mouse might be a better chess player than a human. Think about it, Rosie! What advantage do I have? Smallness. Compactness. While the humans look *down* at the board, I am living inside it.

"Keep playing the Sicilian Defense," Pop said to Gus. His eyes showed deep attentiveness. "She has a better chance of winning with white, but let's see how she reacts."

Gus considered his next move, sticking out the tip of his tongue. Does this help him think? Should I do it? The tip of my tongue darted out.

No, it didn't feel right.

Finally, Gus thunked down another pawn, then sat back.

And I thought about this. What his move meant. How I could respond. Stalling next to the king, I nibbled the end of the bean, which *was* deliciously green. Between the chewing and the thinking, I suddenly realized something. If chess is like a maze, then I should *treat* it like a maze! I should think ten, fifteen, twenty steps ahead—anticipating the roadblocks, the corners, the turns.

I slid my queen to the center of the board.

There!

"Whoa," Gus said, blinking.

Pop whistled a soft, slow tune. "Bold, Clementine. Bold."

Gus leaned forward, fingers steepled under his chin. He chewed his bottom lip. "I guess I'll move my knight . . . here."

In return, I drove my own knight forward.

We fought our way across the board, capturing each other's pieces—until I saw it. A possible pathway to victory. Anticipation fizzed in my chest as I placed my queen just so, checking Gus and his king.

The humans stared at the board for several stunned beats.

Then Pop ran a hand over his face, stifling a huff of laughter. "That's . . . that's checkmate. My! My, oh my. You put up a most excellent fight, Gus, but Clementine . . . Clementine, you are marvelous! I think this is quite a bit more than beginner's luck."

Gus reached out and tipped over his king, resigning. A smile tugged at the corners of his mouth, and he shook his head, letting his glasses slip down his nose. "I'm not imagining this, right?" When he gazed my way, I glanced up at him, whiskers back. "This isn't a dream, right?"

"Well," Pop said, breathing a sigh from his belly, shivering all the hairs of his mustache, "if that's indeed the case, it's a *remarkable* dream."

Always,

Clementine

Letter 15

Dear Rosie,

Here is what a good chess player does. They think many moves ahead.

"Many, *many* moves," Pop said, thumbing a few herbs from his pocket. "A player like Agnes? A master or a grandmaster player? Ten, maybe twelve moves. Maybe the entire game. It takes practice but it also takes something else." His eyes twinkled as he tapped his forehead. "Intuition. Genius. Never in my wildest imagination did I think I'd see that in a mouse."

My chest puffed proudly.

Gus and I played again. And again. I won each round—in fewer than twenty moves. Between games, Pop flitted around the living room, selecting book after book from the shelves. Soon, an enormous stack teetered in his arms, squashing the remaining herbs in his vest. "Here we've got the games of Bobby Fischer. Not the politest man, if you believe the tabloids, but notorious. A stunning player. The thin little book under my chin is a study on endgames. It's elegant. Complex. We also have *Logical Chess: Move by Move*, and . . . Bah! Yes! I have some old books on tape, stashed somewhere in my attic. I . . . buried them. But there's no need to turn the pages! Pages probably get quite heavy, after a while, for a mouse."

He disappeared for almost two hundred seconds, and when he emerged, he plopped a radio-like device next to me, by the armchair. "Tape player," he explained. "And here, all the greats: Garry Kasparov, Alexander Kotov, Bobby Fischer, Mikhail Tal. We don't have much time, but you can listen to them while you're resting, yes?"

Yes! I said, setting up my side of the board again, checkmating Gus soon after. We played on and off for the rest of the day—and afterward, I wanted to extend *them* a kernel of knowledge. So, I spelled out *H-A-M-L-E-T* with the alphabet book, teaching the humans the other mouse's name.

Now it's evening, and I'm writing you this letter. I'm *thinking* you this letter. Unlike last night, there is no mailbox. No postage stamps. It's so strange to be in a new place. I'm not picking the lock on my cage, scampering across the lab.

Are you waiting for me, Rosie?

Are you rattling the bars of your cage?

What do you do with your nights, now that I'm gone?

Maybe you've become friends with a beagle. Maybe a guinea pig has started squeaking to you. I just hope that you're not alone. It's so easy to feel alone in a lab, even when you're surrounded by people.

Will you ever meet Gus? I think he'd recognize the wonder in you. Right now, he's tossing and turning in bed, pillows flattening beneath his head. Over and over, he pushes his blankets down, then pulls them up to his chin. (Blankets! Why didn't the lab have blankets? Something comfortable to curl up in?)

"Clementine?" Gus whispers, his voice big in the dark. "*Pssst.* Are you awake?"

On his nightstand, I lean my shoulder against the terrarium glass, listening.

"I heard that mice are nocturnal," he says, a little louder this time, "but you also weren't making any noise. And the tape player wasn't going anymore. I can switch it to the other side so you can keep listening. It's only halfway through the Queen's Gambit."

To Gus, my whiskers twitch a *yes*.

"Okay," he says, pushing down the blankets once more. "Just give me a second. I can't sleep anyway. I just keep *thinking*."

I know the feeling.

It's nearly impossible to fall asleep when your mind is whirring. Hamlet, on the other hand, has curled himself into a sleeping ball beside me. He'd spent the previous four minutes eyeing the floor, scoping out the box of cereal that Gus had carried up for a nighttime snack. Then, exhausted, he'd instantly begun to snooze, paws twitch-twitching. What does Hamlet dream about? His broken whisker? Reattaching it one day?

"There," Gus says, flipping over the tape. His checkered pajamas glow a little in the moonlight. "The Queen's Gambit is my favorite, I think. People are always expecting it now, but it's hard to counter . . . Did you already listen to the Bobby Fischer tape?"

I nod heartily.

"I've studied all his games, too," Gus says. "Well, not *all* his games. I'm sure he played, like, a million. But all the really famous ones. The championship ones, especially against the Russians. Those guys were all *so* good at chess." He pauses, grabbing his binoculars and lacing the strap around his neck. "Since we're both awake, do you maybe . . . do you want to share binoculars?"

I don't understand.

My head cocks to the right.

"Like . . . check out the garden at night and stuff," he

says. "See what there is to see. It's kind of like a puzzle: figuring out what happens when no one's up to watch it. Wanna look?" Delicately, his fingers curl around my feet, he lifts me from the terrarium, and I join him by the window. "Maybe you can sit on my shoulder?"

So I do.

Oh! Look at me, sitting on a shoulder!

It's like being in a pocket, Rosie. Only taller. And less snug.

I balance there, right by his ear.

"Here, you can look through the right one and I'll look through the left." At first I think he's talking about his ear, so I peer inside it. So holey! So vast! "Hey, that tickles! I meant the binoculars, you goof."

That makes infinitely more sense!

As he holds them up, my nose presses to the lens. Moonlight filters through. And trees! And leaves! Incredibly large leaves, with such fine details. You could see most of the garden from here—even the smallest parts of it. The mouse-size parts of it.

"I bet it's like a whole world to you," he says. "I've always kind of wondered what it'd be like to be *super* tiny. You're kind of small. One of Pop's teacups is like the size of a bathtub to you. And you could sail down a river on a leaf." He mimes the water. *"Sploosh! Zoom."*

But I'm stuck on a question: Why would I want to sail down a river on a leaf?

"Even my friends don't know this," he chatters, "but when I was a kid—like, a baby—I was born pretty early. And I was really, really small. But I don't remember it. And I don't think I could ever fit into a teacup . . . Hey, you're really easy to talk to. You know that?"

From this angle, he can't see my face—my expressive whiskers, the wideness of my eyes. So I gently tug at his earlobe for a *thank-you*.

He chuckles.

Chuckling is another wonderful sound.

Simultaneously, we crane our necks, turning to the street. A bright-white truck flashes by on the other side of the lens. "That's really weird," Gus mumbles. Then to me: "I've seen that truck go by, like, ten times today. It's an ice cream truck. Did you see the menu on the side? Cookie dough and birthday cake sandwiches, and—who'd want ice cream in the middle of the night?"

He bites his lip, thinking.

I try that. I imagine that I look like Hamlet, with his overbite.

"It's probably nothing," Gus says, sweeping a hand through his already-messy hair. "Right? This is the kind of stuff that could get me into trouble. Remember I said

I got into trouble at school? At recess, someone dared me to jump off the top of the swings—and I did. Then my teacher gave me detention because it was a 'dangerous act.' And *then* I got the giggles in detention, so my teacher gave me even more detention. You should've seen the look on my dad's face." A hint of sadness creeps into Gus's voice. "Do you ever get that feeling in your stomach? Like you're thinking all these thoughts, and you feel so guilty that it hurts?"

I consider this, blinking.

Yes. Yes, I suppose I do.

"When my dad picked me up from detention," Gus says, clutching his belly again, "he said I had 'a mind of my own.' I keep thinking about that. Like even my mind is a bad thing." He peers at me. "Maybe we can make a pact, Clementine? No trouble!"

In a flash, Gus reaches out his hand. It hovers there.

"You're supposed to put your paw in," he explains, "if you want in."

Oh! Yes!

I touch my front toes to his thumb, reveling in the feeling. The togetherness. I like him, Rosie.

"Cool," he says. "Okay, forget about the ice cream truck. But I *am* hungry now. You want a snack?"

I don't know the sign for *snack*, or how to express *snack*, so I just think *snack, snack, snack* over and over again—hoping this transfers. It does.

Gus carries me on his shoulder to the kitchen.

So here we are, by the lucky-teacup cabinet. A roll of tinfoil glimmers in the darkness. The refrigerator light buzzes as Gus opens the door with one hand, and—*brussels sprouts!* In the fridge! Surrounded by pure coldness. Green shells tempting me. It's all I can do not to spring from his shoulder, not to weave my way past the orange juice and the butter. *Butter? What does butter taste like?*

"You like noodles?" Gus asks, sealing the pathway to the refrigerator and grabbing two plates. "I think I read that mice can eat pasta? I've been looking stuff up for you. Just to be safe. And responsible." He pauses, a few tufts of hair sticking straight up from his forehead. "When this is all over, and you're totally safe, do you think you'll want to stay here? Or maybe . . . or maybe you can come and live with me?"

He sets me on the counter, where I watch him from the seat of a matchbook. *Live with Gus?* My heart pulses and clenches at the same time. I'm still adjusting to the idea, Rosie—of living away from you.

"You don't have to say yes or no, not right now. I've just been thinking, I have all these miniature ships that you

104

can play with, and I can build you Lego sets, and we have a garden, too. It's smaller than Pop's—much smaller—but we can pick you fresh strawberries and stuff. And we can play chess whenever you want—and do other puzzles, too! I have loads of puzzles. Like Rubik's Cubes! I love Rubik's Cubes! You ever solved one?"

I shake my head, intrigued.

"Oh, wow, we've gotta do that, then. We can hang out at the park and get you a tiny canoe for the pool, and Pop doesn't live that far away, either, so you could still see him. I come over all the time in the school year, and for all the holidays . . . Want to know something?"

Yes! I curl up on the spot, forepaws cradling my chin. *Knowledge is good. I like knowledge.*

"Sometimes I like it better here than at my own house." Sighing, Gus splits a bowl of noodles between two plates. "I'm just . . . I'm trying my best."

He blinks—and his eyes say, *You know?*

I do.

I do know.

A good lab mouse tries her best, too.

"I'm sorry I haven't told you this yet," he says, pushing the smaller plate toward me, "but I had no idea about all the animals in labs. *No* idea. I'm really, really sorry that the lab is trying to . . . you know . . . get you and stuff. For what it's worth, I think your brain's much better inside your head."

He catches my gaze. I catch his.

Rosie? I think I've found another friend.

Always,

Clementine

Letter 16

Dear Rosie,

Whenever I fell asleep in the lab, even for three seconds, I'd dream of the maze. All zigzags and crisscrosses. Except I couldn't get out. Each turn was the wrong one, and I kept circling back on myself. The pathways would narrow, walls collapsing, until plastic pressed against my fur.

Then the dream would end.

Outside the lab, I thought it would be the same. But it wasn't. After Gus carried me back upstairs, I dreamed, there on the nightstand, of sunflowers blooming inside me. I dreamed that the entire world was a chessboard. And I was weaving through it.

From the edge of the board, you were watching me— eyes warm, grinning your chimp grin. You were cheering on the game with a *hoot*.

(That's all! I just wanted to tell you something good.)

Always,

Clementine

Letter 17

Dear Rosie,

As I said, in these letters, I might not be able to tell you everything. Because I might not *remember* to tell you everything. Just the big moments. Just the times that stick in my brain—the bright, flashing beacons.

Like . . . pockets! Let me tell you more about pockets, Rosie! From the terrarium, Gus scooped me up, then slipped me into the pouch of his vest. "I borrowed one of Pop's," he explained. "Because I haven't done laundry in forever. Also, I don't know how to do laundry. You think it's too big?"

From inside the pocket, my front legs dangled over the fabric ledge. I looked down to see the edge of the vest reach past his knees. *Perfect!* I nodded vigorously.

"Okay," Gus said. "Thanks."

We clomped downstairs as I thought, *Here I am with my friend.* And also: *So this is what it's like to be tall.* And at the same time: *Don't poop. Never poop in a pocket.*

Huh? Hamlet said, in the terrarium clutched low in Gus's arms. He was just emerging from slumber. *Huh? Hello?*

Good morning! It's morning! I said, wiggling my tail in the pocket.

Pop said a variation of the same thing just as he glimpsed the three of us. "*Kaliméra*, my friends!" Behind him, coffee was boiling in a tall, narrow pot. "I would offer you some," he said politely, "but I'm afraid it's very strong. I've had four cups myself this morning, so I'm beginning to feel like Clementine! Buzzing all over the chessboard! Good morning, Clementine."

With one finger, he rubbed me delicately under the chin.

Oooh, that was nice!

A nice feeling.

In the background, underneath the whistling of the coffee pot, was another noise. The radio.

> . . . that means, you know, that everyone is still on the lookout for Wondermouse. You think she's living on her own, or that someone's hiding her? They upped the reward money. The lab's knocking on everyone's door, and if I remember correctly,

they're bringing in those dogs today. Those
scent-sniffing dogs? I wonder if—

"I think that's enough for now," Pop said kindly and delicately, reaching over to turn off the radio. "Especially when eggs are on the menu, hmm? Anyone care for eggs?"

As a matter of fact, Rosie, I did.

I'd never had eggs before.

But I had a suspicion I'd appreciate them. Eggs! Delicious eggs! There is something about eggs that makes you think of nothing but eggs. Eggs!

"Clementine," Pop said, eyes twinkling. "Would you pass the oregano?"

Me?

"Yes. Yes, you. The little green vial to your left. Right there."

I jumped to the counter and pushed the vial toward him like a chess piece, like a queen or a rook. He crushed the herbs in his palms, adding them to the eggs.

"Thank you," Pop said. "Now, I've been mulling it over. What exactly does a mouse need to know about playing chess?" He set aside the spatula and counted on his fingers, peering down at me. "One, how to think ahead. Two, how to carry yourself in the game. And three, how to read your opponent's moves."

I blinked at each of the suggestions. *Think ahead! Carry myself! Read!* I could do that! Yes! And I was listening to him. I was listening until that tinfoil glimmered, once more, by the refrigerator. Inching back slowly, I bit off a piece, shaped it, and flattened my ears. The little hat fit straight over my head. I'd missed it! I never should've taken it off! No, it wasn't much protection for my brain, but didn't it match the grayness of my fur?

Snug, Hamlet said.

I whipped around to see him—in the terrarium, on the breakfast table. Did I hear that right? *Snug*? Did he say something other than *huh*?

Gus broke me from my thoughts as he cracked an egg. "Okay! Okay, that's good." He cracked another one, half of the eggshell splitting into the bowl. "Darn it! Sorry. I'm sorry."

"It's okay," Pop said. "It's just an egg. Eggs are made for breaking."

Gus let out a long breath. "Okay . . . But no mazes. I know that's thinking ahead, but we shouldn't do that here. I don't want her to go back to anything like the lab."

"Certainly not!" Pop assured me, a tiny grin curling his

mustache when he glimpsed my hat. It hugged my ears so wonderfully. "I was thinking more like . . ." He trailed off, color suddenly draining from his face. "Where is the other mouse?"

My heart jumped.

My neck swiveled again.

Hamlet was no longer in the terrarium.

Hamlet is gone!

Always,

Clementine

Letter 18

Dear Rosie,

Gone, as you know, is an important word. I didn't have the chance to say goodbye to Hamlet. Or howl like you. Now I'm shivering here on the countertop, my tinfoil hat shaking, wondering, *Where are you, Hamlet? Where?* I scan the floor, peering into dusty corners, dread slowly creeping up my tail.

Is this how you felt, Rosie, after I was gone?

"My word!" yells Pop, clapping a hand to his forehead. The sound is a giant *smack*. "We are reasonably intelligent people, my Gus! How do we keep losing these mice?"

I quiver, starting to panic. My heartbeat triples.

But then we hear a tiny *munch, munch* from a cereal box on the kitchen counter. Gus says, "Phew," gently dumping out Hamlet—who's stuffed his cheeks to the brim with Cheerios. From his back, legs happily in the air, Hamlet seems to wink at me.

And a memory arrives.

Rosie, I'd like to tell you something about Hamlet.

After the researchers discovered that the experiment had worked, that I might be the smartest mouse in history, they started placing me in the maze with other mice. "Let's see if she'll guide them through," one of the researchers said. "It's worth a try. Maybe she'll help." I'd wait at the entrance, my tail softly curled behind me—greeting the other mice with a wave.

Hello!

This way.

It was an interesting challenge. Sometimes I'd jump in front of them, saying, *Follow my lead*. Other times they were more skittish, and I'd trail behind them, offering encouragement. *Good, excellent, almost there!* One of the mice—tiny and gray, with enormous ears—even asked to squeeze by my side. We rounded the corners, paw-step for paw-step.

Hamlet was in a category of his own.

When the researchers dropped him in front of me, each one of his whiskers was pulled back, his nose trembling. Before I could say anything, he jumped and planted all four paws against the smooth walls of the maze. Didn't he understand the point of the exercise? Why was he suspended like that, a tail's-width above the ground?

This way, I told him.

Eventually, he dropped to the floor—then sped

immediately in the other direction. I watched his hind-quarters skitter around the corner. The heart-shaped spot, just above his tail, stared back. *Incredible*, I thought. *I have a spot like that, too.*

What he lacked in intelligence, Hamlet made up for in speed.

I followed him in circles, whizzing around the maze.

Every once in a while, without warning, he'd stop. He'd plant his paws and refuse to budge. In some corners of the maze, the researchers had placed a snack. A small crumb of cheese. A pumpkin seed. Little rewards to help us navigate the route. Hamlet would race up to the food, shove it hungrily into his mouth, and then whirl around, scurrying down the wrong path again.

At my best, I could complete the maze in 10.7 seconds. After an hour and twenty-six minutes, one of the researchers pulled Hamlet out. "I don't think it's going to happen," he said. "He can't make a good choice to save his life."

So they placed Hamlet back in his cage.

Our cage.

Now that I think about it, Rosie, maybe Hamlet is smarter than anyone gives him credit for. The longer he failed at the maze, the longer he was free.

Always,

Clementine

Letter 19

Dear Rosie,

Right now, I am free. Freedom tastes of eggs. Hard-boiled eggs. I nibble on a smidge as Pop sets up the chessboard.

"I think it's time we play each other, Clementine," he says, corralling his white hair into a bun, "so you get the chance to face a variety of opponents. Agnes is a far more skilled player than I, especially at speed chess . . . but don't let my age fool you! Or my time off. I'm still quite quick." He winks at me and stretches out the backs of his hands, which are shaking again—just a touch. "I promise not to go easy on you, little mouse. That won't do anyone any good. Shall we?"

I swallow a bit of egg and nod, whiskers perked.

He's going to play me? Really?

This is special. I know it in my tail. At the same time, I wonder: Why'd he quit? Why'd he quit the game, all those years ago?

After removing a pair of dark-green spectacles from his vest and placing them on the very tip of his nose, Pop moves first: a pawn to e6.

"That's e6," he says, tip-tapping the checkered square. His voice is always so musical, so uplifting! "All the squares have names, just like all the pieces have names. You listened to your chess books last night, yes? So you probably know this already. But if not, it's spectacular for you to learn: *a* through *h* along this side, 1 through 8 along this side, and then we match them up." His finger trails diagonally across the board. "Here's a1, b2, c3. See? That's chess notation. Simple! Now you go."

Wiping the egg from my paws, I go—back legs strong against the board. Push, push, pushing a pawn, out in front of my king.

Pop settles back in the armchair with a grin, curling the ends of his mustache. "The French Defense? Ha! So clever, Clementine."

"What'd I miss?" asks Gus, trotting in from the kitchen, a gigantic plate of eggs in his hands. Eagerly, he plops down on the floor, legs crossed, eyes level with the board. "Wait, you're playing her?" Gus's eyes can't contain his disbelief—or his joy.

"Our mouse is learning very fast," Pop says, clearly pleased.

Our mouse.

The way he says it perks my whiskers even more. He says it not like they own me, not like I'm *for* them. He says it like I'm *with* them.

"Right, right, right," Pop mumbles over the board. "Now . . . this!"

He moves.

I move.

He moves.

I move.

And a strange thing begins to happen, Rosie. I start to think way, *way* ahead. I start to see all the dead ends and the possibilities, every turn that Pop might take. To me, the board has always been a maze, but this is the first time I can picture it: how I might get *all the way* to the other side.

"Bah!" Pop says at my eighth move. He taps a thumb against his lips. A strange thing is happening with him, too, Rosie. It's like he's been sleeping. And now he's waking up. "I didn't consider that, but yes . . . Yes, little mouse. Excellent, excellent."

Safe in his terrarium (with an extra mesh lid on it this time), Hamlet watches from a shelf near the fireplace, belly expanded with twelve and a half Cheerios. For three seconds, he rocks back on his tail, feet in the air—and then curls into a ball, observing us peacefully.

"The first time I sat down at a chessboard, I was just a boy," Pop says, wiping a hand across his face. His words seem very close but also very far away. "That was over sixty years ago. Over sixty years of chess, Clementine. Even in my off time, even in the years I've been away, I've been dreaming about it. And I have never—and I mean never—encountered a player like you. Not even in my daydreams. The fact that you are already this good, after two days, is extraordinary."

"You think . . ." Gus says worriedly, through a mouthful of eggs. "You think she might be okay against Agnes?"

Pop dips his head once. "She'll stand a chance. Oh yes."

A chance. *Chance* is another important word, Rosie. Lab animals rarely get one.

He moves.

I move.

We battle back and forth as I tuck my tail, weaving through the pieces. Finally, he brings his queen to capture my last rook, and my king is exposed. I drag out a knight to protect it . . . but it's too late. Pop swoops in with a bishop, checkmating me.

Oh. Oh, I see.

What a brilliant game he's played!

"I'm sorry, little mouse," Pop says, voice soothing. "The

exceptional news is, you're a real chess player now! Every player I've ever known has lost in the beginning. You learn so much from failure. I bet you won't trade away your bishop in that scenario again, will you?" He reaches out to tip my chin up with a single finger. "There we go. Hold your head high. Now, again?"

We play once more. Twice more. Three times. And I *am* learning! I'm learning so much from Pop, from these losses. Our final game stretches longer and longer—and eventually, when my heart begins to pitter-patter so fast that I'm wobbling on the board, Pop suggests, "Do you want to adjourn? Seal your move and give yourself a rest? Let's do that. It's such a beautiful day. I imagine that you haven't seen many beautiful days, Clementine. Shall we finish the game in the greenhouse?"

Greenhouse! A house full of green! Heart pattering, I imagine towers of brussels sprouts and bushels of leafy leaves and carrots and—

"Won't someone see us outside?" Gus asks, nervously tugging one of the holes in his jeans.

"Ha!" Pop counters. "Not if we take the secret way!"

So we scurry through the sunflower stalks, through the dense apple orchard, through a pathway of hanging vines. Hamlet sways in the terrarium as Pop carries him alongside the alphabet book, and soon, so quick, we're in the greenhouse. Which is exactly how it sounds! Warm green light filters through the glass. Soft leaves spill from planters. There are tomatoes! And more tomatoes! And soil!

"You can take a look around," Gus says slowly, setting me down by a potted plant. "Just be really careful."

Oh! I will!

So careful! Carefully leaping into this pot full of tomatoes. Carefully *tasting* a tomato. Then another. Then another. Then another. Then another. Then—

Pop laughs his full-bodied laugh. "She is a mouse of many interests."

Still chewing, I watch as they reset the board on a small, wobbly table—right next to a coil of garden hose.

"Know what would be interesting to consider?" Pop asks, green light filtering onto his shoulders. "How you see the pieces, Clementine. I hadn't read a chess book in over a decade—yet I'm reading a book right now, about a young chess prodigy, much like you. She pictures all the pieces on the ceiling."

"Weren't you a prodigy?" Gus asks Pop.

"No, no," Pop says firmly, with a bit more edge than customary. Brushing off the question, he points to the green glass above us, and I crane my neck to see. "Truly! Up there. She plays whole games from her bed, in her imagination, just watching the pieces move upside down."

"That's cool," Gus says, laying out the pawns. He seems a touch wounded by Pop's *no*. "This is going to sound stupid, but . . . I kind of think that all the pieces have personalities? Like, the knight is really brave."

"That's not stupid," Pop says seriously. "That is far from stupid."

"Okay," Gus says, gaining a bit more energy. "Well, the rook feels sorry for everyone when they're captured. And the bishop kind of . . . kind of reminds me of Aunt Susan."

I jump when Pop slaps his knee. "Yes! Susan! On your mother's side? Oh, I can envision that perfectly. Every time I've met her, she's always had the same facial expression. And she can never seem to remember the name Kristo. She calls me *Crisco*. Or *Krispy*. Like I'm fried in oil!"

This makes Gus giggle.

Which makes *me* feel like giggling, too. Because I'm happy, Rosie! I'm happy to be here with them, with tomato juice dripping down my whiskers.

"What about you, Clementine?" Pop asks. "What do you think about?"

At this point, Hamlet perks up in the terrarium, waiting for my response. Everyone is waiting for my response.

Gus opens the alphabet book, and soon, letters shimmer under my tomatoey paws. What to say? How to tell them what I see? How to tell them that here, the world is smaller? More comfortable? Mouse-size? Here, the world exists in a series of squares. Whenever I play, I want to climb atop my rook and teeter, taking in the whole board. The kingdom. A place where I am no longer just a lab mouse.

"R," Gus says, watching me flit.

"O," Pop says.

"S-I-E," Gus finishes, confused. His eyes are soft as he peers down at me. "Who's Rosie?"

I blink at him.

And think about you, Rosie.

I think about all the words you taught me—still there, looping in the back of my brain. *Hello, apple, sad, mouse, home.* The last one is especially sticky.

Home. Home. Home.

Rosie. Rosie, how long have you lived at the lab? Way before I was born? Before the beagles and the guinea pigs? Were you always an Inside Chimpanzee? For the last two days, I've been trying to piece it together. All the things I know about you. All the things that are missing.

But—

I clamp my ears shut. With both paws. Squeezing

tight. Because suddenly, I hear it. Your howl again. You're howling again.

And it's still the loudest sound I've ever heard.

It's just a memory.

Only a memory!

Yet, here's the thing about brain-pictures, about brain-sounds. They're as real as chess pieces. They're as solid as a rook.

"Whoa, Clementine," Gus says, voice coated with worry. He bends down to his knees, nose inches from my face. "What's wrong? Are you okay?"

But the howl is too loud. Too loud. Too—

Curling up on the spot, I settle myself against the *E*. It isn't the same as being close to you, Rosie. But it's something. It's—

Hamlet.

Hamlet?

Still in the terrarium, by the chessboard, he's pressing his paws to the glass. Like he's trying to escape for me, get to me, embrace me.

Like he knows what I spelled.

Always,

Clementine

Dear Rosie,

Three things happened next.

I will put them in three individual letters—to store them tidily in my memory.

Ready?

The first thing is we finished our chess game. I pinned Pop's rook in the corner, and he captured my queen. For almost an hour, the two of us circled each other on the board, chasing kings with bishops and pawns. Finally, Pop blew out a gust of air and grinned. "I think this is a draw, Clementine. And I . . . I haven't finished in a draw since midway through my career. Perhaps, just maybe, I've met my match." His warm eyes glowed. "A draw against a former champion is nothing to sniff at, little mouse. You can be proud of this."

I was!

So proud that, in celebration, I hopped down from the

table, tried to crawl into the garden hose, and got stuck. Very stuck. Very, very stuck.

Gus fished me out, gentle as ever.

Always,

Clementine

Dear Rosie,

The second thing is, we worked on my TV camera presence.

The humans placed me on the dining room table by the spice shakers. Don't sniff pepper, Rosie. That's my recommendation. And don't eat salt. Bleh! You *should* taste sugar, though. Casually lifting the lid, my front toes licked up the sweetness—crystal by crystal. As I was sugar-tasting, a thoughtful look passed over Gus's face. He ducked upstairs, perhaps into his bedroom, and started rummaging around. I heard the *thump-thump* of his sneakers. "Here, Clementine," he said, returning forty seconds later, a shiny object in his hand. "Maybe this can help? It's a pocket mirror. If you stand back a little, you can see yourself!"

Ooooh! Oh! Scurrying up to the mirror, I sniffed the scentless glass. My nose smudged against it. *Oh. Hi. That's me.* It was the first time I'd actually paused to see my reflection. Was my head really that large? Were my paws really that small? It was so strange! On my hind legs, I took a few steps back, examining myself from all angles. *There is my tail. There is my spot.*

"Do you know," Pop said, a sly smile spreading across his face, "for my big chess tournaments, I used to practice keeping a straight face in the mirror? I didn't have this glorious mustache back then! My face revealed everything. Whether I'd maneuvered my piece poorly. Whether I'd made a move I was proud of." He laughed a Pop laugh. "I'm happy not to worry about that anymore. Imagine if my face never moved on the show!"

Gazing up at him, I thought: *If I were Pop, I'd walk with a bounce in my step.*

I tried that in the mirror.

If I were Pop, I'd pick a hat from a tree branch.

I mimed that, too.

"Oh, you're good," Gus said. "People are going to love you."

I hope so, a voice inside me said. *My life depends on it.*

Always,

Clementine

Dear Rosie,

The third thing happened that night. It's shocking, Rosie. Prepare yourself.

"It says here on my phone that mice are really clean," Gus whispered. He was sitting up in bed, ankles crossed, darkness coating his green pajamas. Electronic light washed over his face. "I can tell you're really clean, too. And it says rats are ticklish? Is that true? I know you're not a rat! Sorry if I just . . . insulted you or something?"

Rats are kind, I tried to convey with my eyes. *Guinea pigs, too! And rabbits.*

He acknowledged this with a head bob, then kept scrolling. "It also says that all mice have facial expressions, like you did in the mirror . . . 'If mice are happy or scared, they'll show it.' Well, duh! It seems like researchers would've found this out a long time ago if they'd just *asked* the mice. Or noticed."

Gus twisted to the side, pillow under his head. His

pupils were rather large as he gazed at me in the terrarium, like he was thinking hard. When he spoke again, his voice was quiet as a mouse. "Was it awful?"

Was what awful?

"The lab. I looked it up on Google. Some of the experiments are . . . *bad.* It's like a puzzle that I can't figure out: how people can do this stuff to animals. And then I googled a few other labs, and those are even worse. Much, much worse. It's hard to look at that stuff. Some of those pictures gave me the worst stomachache I've ever had. It makes me so angry. *Really* mad. You shouldn't have to play chess to save yourself. You never should've been in that place at all."

He rubbed a corner of his eye, like a tear was about to fall from it.

My belly sank. And my heart thrummed.

"One day," he said, "after you win the chess match on TV and you're totally free, you can tell me about your life in the lab. If you want to. Because I'll listen."

Just like I did on the first day, he cupped both hands behind his ears. He held my gaze.

I held his.

Inside the terrarium, I pressed one paw against the glass, thanking him. Because I would like to share with him, one day. These letters inside my mind. They are for you, Rosie—but maybe they can also be for Gus? Maybe letters can have more than one reader.

And Hamlet!

Would you understand them, Hamlet?

Behind me, he nestled himself into a thick pile of moss; he was cuddling a button. Somehow, there were new items in the terrarium: three tiny blue buttons, a growing pile of woodchips, and a hammock. A mouse-size hammock suspended between two miniature ferns. Did Gus hang it there?

Should I swing on it?

Yes!

Eventually Gus switched off his glowing blue lamp, and the whole room plunged into blackness. Shadows inched across the terrarium's mossy floor. One of the side effects of the experiment is I barely sleep. But maybe all that non-sleep had caught up to me. Still listening to Pop's books on tape, I snuggled into the hammock. Chess strategies hummed in the background: *If you're going to formulate a plan before the match, remember to think about forks, pins, and skewers.* I'd just . . . curl up . . . for a second or two . . .

Before I could even think *sleep*, I was snoozing. My whiskers relaxed. My heart rate slowed. Dreamy Latin phrases began unrolling in my mind. *Ego amare caseus. Et ova. Et lamminis argenteis pullulat sunt.*

Around midnight, though, there was a noise.

Pffft, pffft. Quick feet over moss.

My eyes twitched open, half slits in the moonlight.

Is that? Is that right?

Before turning off the lights, Gus had placed the pocket mirror in the terrarium. I thought I glimpsed Hamlet by it now, fashioning a scarf out of moss. He'd peeled a long layer of it and was draping it around his shoulders. The scarf fell over his gray tufts of fur, stopping just above his tail. Could Hamlet really be twirling in front of the mirror, checking his reflection from all sides? *Huh*, I thought I heard him say, before I forced myself back to sleep. It would all make sense in the morning.

Except, in the middle of the night, it was even more confusing.

Gus gasped, a few drops from his water glass sloshing to the floor. He'd come up from the kitchen, I think, and his footsteps had startled me awake. I popped my head up from the hammock and saw what Hamlet had done. Immediately, a sound began to bleat between my ears—dizzying me.

"*Whoa,*" Gus burst out, peering into the terrarium. Dark tufts of hair stuck up all around his head, and his eyes were both heavy with sleep and fully round. "Is that . . . ? Is that a miniature replica of Notre Dame Cathedral?"

Yes.

Yes, it is.

Hamlet had sculpted a masterpiece out of wood-chips. Two colossal towers flanked the building, which extended more than halfway up the terrarium glass. For a mouse resting right beside it, the building was dizzy-ingly tall—and you could see all the fine details, all the love he'd stamped into the structure. The complex series of half arches. The little galleries. The intricate carvings above mouse-size doorways. Had he etched those with his teeth?

As I stared at Hamlet's handiwork, the bleating sound grew and grew in my mind, knocking me further off bal-ance. No one else could hear it. It was just me, Rosie. Just my brain, shifting something. Something that made sense and yet made no sense at all. I blinked and blinked, watching Hamlet. On the far side of a succulent, he was eyeing his creation, paws on his hips. His scarf had gotten chunkier somehow; it wrapped thickly around his neck. The building towered above him, made entirely of wood-chips and . . . glue?

"I thought I heard a minor cacophony," Pop said, tum-bling into the room. When he flicked on the lights, his hair was almost circular, like a halo. He was wearing a bathrobe—which is similar to a lab coat, yet fluffier.

Shuffling over in his gigantic slippers, he came to stand right next to Gus, words failing him as he spied the cathedral.

"I got thirsty," Gus finally managed in little more than a whisper. "I couldn't sleep so I was playing with my binoculars, and I got thirsty, and when I came back up from the kitchen, I noticed . . . *Wow*. I noticed this." He caught my glance. "Where'd you even get that glue? I mean, I guess you could've climbed up the fern, bounced out, taken it from the desk, used that bonsai tree like a tiny ladder . . . Clementine, this is so cool!"

Me?

My toes jittered with realization.

They think I *built this!*

Oblivious to their conversation, Hamlet took a step back, cocking his ears. *Huh*, he said to the building. Only this time, it sounded more like *I am pleased with this work*.

Did you ever see it, Rosie? The poster by Felix's desk? Hamlet never sat dreamily by the edge of our cage, paws tucked under his chin, gazing out at the poster. But he must've absorbed the picture somehow: a cathedral, bathed in light.

There! Those turrets. The spire.

There was even a miniature gargoyle guarding the roof.

Frantically, I slipped from the hammock, scampering

to Hamlet's side. He'd lost a small patch of fur in the night. A bald spot gleamed right behind his left ear. Examining his paws, I realized that—at some point during the last several hours—he'd glued his toes to his fur.

A small price to pay, I guess.

The two of us stood in the shadow of the cathedral.

Or maybe it stood in the shadow of us.

"Look at those wonderful little church bells," Pop mused, tilting his head to gaze inside the structure. "Gargoyle? Are those *gargoyles*, Clementine?"

No. I shook my head, ears jittering, and pointed at Hamlet. *Him. Him. Him!* Over and over, my tail gestured between Hamlet and the cathedral.

Finally, Gus's eyes widened farther than I'd ever seen. "Pop! It's him! The other mouse! Hamlet built this!"

Pop jolted, his hair blowing back in realization. "Bah!"

Breathe, my mind told me, like it did the second I was born. My nose fluttered.

But my heart hurt. Physically hurt, Rosie.

Something was occurring to me. Something was working its way up my tail.

"How is this possible?" Gus asked, fingers pressing into his temples. He leaned forward, sniffing. "He smells like raspberries now, too! I thought that the experiment didn't work with him?"

I blink-blink-blinked at Gus, at Hamlet—back and forth and back and forth.

It didn't work! It hadn't worked! And yet . . . it did.

Through the bush of his eyebrows, Pop studied Hamlet's handiwork, then looked at me. "It must be . . . a delayed reaction." His voice filled with worry. "You must've had the strongest and earliest response to the experiment, Clementine, but there might be others. Other mice that are gaining superintelligence and have yet to show any signs. My word! Perhaps they will soon."

Did you see it? Hamlet asked me then, looking expectantly in my direction. *My castle?*

And I tell him, *Yes. Yes. Yes.*

Each *yes* was softer. Because I was wilting, Rosie. Wilting.

If the researchers wanted *my* brain, what about the other four mice? What if they started showing signs of superintelligence? Weren't they in danger, too?

Even worse danger, my mind said. *They're still in the lab.*

Always,

Clementine

Letter 21

Dear Rosie,

Have you met the other mice in the lab, Rosie?

They were good lab mice, the ones I left behind. They ran drills and ate pellets and did their best for science.

Beyond that, they were kind.

Are they more intelligent now? Do they visit you nightly in the darkness of your cage?

I have so many wishes. So many things I would've said and done—if I'd only known I was leaving. And maybe . . . maybe one of them should've been to tell you, Rosie: *Get to know the mice*. I never really did that with Hamlet. All I needed was you.

These letters that I'm writing to you are only imaginary.

They aren't letters you can chew. But right now, staring at Hamlet's cathedral, I have another wish: Make them real. Send a bundle to you. Say, *Rosie? Rosie! If you see a mouse in the lab, please tell her to run.*

"Wait a second," Gus said, voice queasy. He gulped at

me. "Are there other mice? Because if there are . . . will the researchers kill those mice, too? For their brains?"

Gulping, too, I turned to face Hamlet, our tails almost touching. I raised my forepaw in a slow wave, like we were meeting for the first time.

He did the same.

My tail perked.

His perked, too.

Titling my head to the left, I watched him follow, reflecting my every move. *Is he mirroring me?* Delicately, I lifted one leg into the air, balancing on my toes—and he shadowed the movement.

I blinked.

He blinked.

And I understood. I understood what he was telling me, Rosie. That we're the same. That we've always been the same. Hasn't he been helping me all along? Didn't he escape the terrarium so that I could find him and learn?

Suddenly, Hamlet scurried toward the food dish, rooting around through the seeds. He seemed to be on a mission. Every once in a while, a pumpkin seed flew over his shoulder. One of them bopped me in the head.

Finally, *pffft, pffft.* Mouse feet over moss.

In his paws was a geometrically perfect sunflower seed.

No chips. No dents. *Huh*, he said, giving it to me—and I took it, holding the gift close to my chest.

You're here, his eyes said, *and I'm here, and we're here together.*

At least we have that.

Always,
Clementine

Letter 22

Dear Rosie,

Hamlet slept the rest of the night tucked inside his cathedral. The tip of his tail dangled from the oversize window. After what had happened, it was hard for me to believe that anyone could return to sleep. The other mice! The danger! Weren't we all feeling it? Didn't it frighten us? (Or was everyone more optimistic than me?)

"I can't stand it!" Gus erupted right before the sun rose. He tossed the sheets off his legs, making his binoculars flop to the floor. "I've just been lying here all night, thinking about those mice, and every time I close my eyes, I see them. I haven't even met them, but I can picture their cute little faces, and their whiskers, and I know Pop said that—besides breaking into the lab—there's nothing we can do right now. We just have to keep going with chess. And I *know* he said we'd talk about it in the morning, but we need to do *something*, right?"

I nodded vigorously while springing from the hammock.

Chess is still the way! I believe that, Rosie. On live TV, I can offer proof that the experiment had worked, proof that our brains are better *inside* our heads. But I need to accelerate my learning! Step up my game! Instead of playing for myself, to stay alive (and keep the hope of one day seeing you again), I'll be competing for all of us.

So I jiggled some more, adding my tail for emphasis.

"I feel like I know *exactly* what you're thinking," Gus said to me, rifling through the dresser to find a clean shirt. I watched as laundry flew. Laundry was flung. Two T-shirts, flying through the air! "It's actually freaking me out a little. But yeah, it's bigger now. The whole thing's bigger. So we need to get much better at chess—and *fast*."

Fast! I could be fast.

"You haven't won any games against Pop yet," Gus said, peering back at me, eyes wide under his glasses. He'd just replaced the frayed silver tape with glue (the glue that Hamlet found!). "You got that one draw, but it's still a problem. Pop's a *great* player. If you can't beat him, though, you might never beat Agnes . . . Don't feel bad! I know what's going on. You haven't played enough people. Really, really good people. The more opponents, the better you'll get. That's how I got better. By playing some of my aunts at Easter. That makes sense, right? Right!" Gus's voice approached a screech as he finished. He barely waited for my response, dashing out of the room in his socks.

Hello?

Hello?

"Okay!" he bellowed, returning fifty seconds later. "Pop's asleep. Like, *asleep.* I tried to wake him—three times—but I've heard bears with quieter snores. So we just need to go now. If we don't leave soon, we'll miss the start. I googled it! You ready?"

Go? Go where? The start of what? Questions flitted into my brain. Whiskers still droopy with sleep, Hamlet followed this up with: *Eggs? Egg? Eggs?*

Quickly, Gus shrugged on one of Pop's gardening vests. "Do you trust me?"

I realized, with a bright *ping* between my ears, that I did.

"Thank you," Gus said, dipping his chin. Then he got to work. "I think I can bike there in about twelve minutes if we leave right away—but first, two things." He carried the terrarium into the bathroom, then placed Hamlet and me on the sink basin and creaked open a glass cabinet. "Nope, not soap, not deodorant, not poison ivy cream. Here!"

Gus selected three square bottles.

One by one, he sprayed the contents all over himself: in his hair, under his arms, across his back. The scent, Rosie! Those smells! Like wood and chemicals and fruit and—

"Pop's old cologne is *strong*," Gus said, coughing. Coughing. One more cough. "But it'll mask some of the raspberry smell. Now, if anyone *sees* either of you, we'll obviously be in big trouble. You'll have to stay in my pocket. Don't peek out!"

Hamlet's eyes widened, as if to say, *I would never.*

To accentuate the point, he sneezed.

"Bless you," Gus said, tapping him lightly on the head. "If all else fails, there's some brown felt in the kitchen. I'll grab it on the way out, and you can drape it over yourselves and say you're guinea pigs. Wow, when I say it out loud, it sounds really stupid." He shook his head. "Never mind. Let's go!"

He pounded down the stairs, Hamlet and me in hand, and then lurched into the outdoors.

In the early-morning sunlight, through the apple trees and the rows of lettuce, stood a bicycle. A bright-green bicycle, with a wicker basket and streamers on the handlebars. "Just hold on tight," Gus said, placing us inside the basket. "Can you cling to the edge? Good!"

More lurching.

Wind sifted through the wicker.

Hamlet had pressed his back against the basket, tail shivering, chest rising and falling. It was easy to tell that he preferred the terrarium. In here, where was the moss?

"I should've tried harder to wake Pop, shouldn't I?" Gus said over the wind. He pedaled faster and faster, weaving through those apple trees, past the mailbox, onto the road. His glasses slipped down with the movement. "Oh no, I should've. What am I *doing*? Oh gosh, I'm messing up right now, aren't I? I just googled the thing, and kept thinking about the other mice, and . . . Should I turn around? Do you think Pop will ever forgive me? I don't want to disappoint him, too! My stomach. My stomach hurts so bad, but . . . You're really great, Clementine! Both of you are my friends! And if those mice are anything like you, I can't let them die!"

For a second, an idea seized me.

Were we headed to the lab?

Was Gus about to break into the lab?

Rosie! Was I about to see you again?

Fear and hope battled in my chest. *No. Yes. Gus! Wait!*

Finding my footing, tiny toes against the wicker, I climbed to the rim of the basket, wind in my fur. Ears back. Whiskers flat against my face, I savored the feeling. (Freedom tastes of eggs, but it also tastes of an early-morning breeze.)

Eventually, the road diverged. We sped left, farther from the lab.

Half my heart went the other way.

"It's this club," Gus said, a touch out of breath now. Movement rippled his grandpa's vest. "A group of people come to Whisper Creek Park every Sunday morning, right after sunrise, and play chess. Anyone's welcome. So I'll play, okay? And you can watch all the moves. I think it'll really help—because you'll learn how to read other people's gestures, and how to get your opponent to do what you want. This might be the biggest mistake I've ever made . . . but I have to try! Remember, just *stay down*."

Near the WHISPER CREEK PARK sign, Gus leaned his bike against a tree, then lined his shirt pocket with a tissue ("For you to hide under, if you need it") and placed us inside. Tissue particles traveled up my nose. Which was wonderful! It lessened the smell of cologne.

Chew? Hamlet asked, passing me a piece of tissue.

Thank you, no thank you, I told him, then peeked through a tiny hole in Gus's borrowed vest, careful to keep our tails out of sight. With our combined weight, I could tell we were sagging the pocket. Hamlet wiggled as he chewed.

Down, I reminded him.

Up! he replied, as if it were a game.

"Youngster!" someone shouted in the distance.

Panicked, I spun my head toward the caller. Through the tiny hole, everything was visible. Tables spread out on the shimmering grass. And chessboards! There were chessboards, a number of humans hunched over them—already engaged in play.

"You there!" the voice repeated. "With the vest! And the pockets! Yes, you! I'm in desperate need of a chess partner. Marty's called in sick today, the old dog. I don't believe a word of it. He's still sore from when I beat him last Sunday. Now, you're not a ringer, are ya?"

Gus tiptoed over to the woman—the oldest human I'd ever seen. Nudging Hamlet aside a little, I blinked through the hole, examining her ears. Her wonderful ears, Rosie! She might be ninety-six. Or ninety-seven. She wore a feathery blue coat, which matched the color of her hair.

"A ringer?" Gus asked, trying not to look down at us. (Which was difficult, I'm sure. Hamlet was jiggling his bottom.)

"You know," the woman continued, gray eyes twinkling, "someone who's come in to beat me, to wipe all the money from my pockets."

Gus gulped. "Uh . . . We're not playing for money, are we, ma'am? I didn't bring any money."

"Not to worry, not to worry. You'll just have to pay me

with secrets." She wiggled her eyebrows up and down, then laughed. "Only kidding. What's your name, young man?"

"Gus."

"And what are the names of the mice in your pocket?"

Hamlet and I stiffened. Gus stiffened. The pace of our heartbeats collectively grew, and none of us—absolutely none of us—knew what to say. Was this it? Had we made a terrible mistake? Would she report our presence to the lab?

Hamlet gripped his whiskers.

I did the same.

Gus had no whiskers of his own to hold on to, but eventually, he found his voice. "They're . . . they're, uh . . ." His pink ears pinked even more. He started to swivel around. "I'm going to go home now. Sorry. Sorry. You won't tell, will you?"

"Bah! Who would I tell? Marty? Marty's afraid of me, remember? Plus, I've seen weirder. I lived in Florida in the nineties." She patted the table with a wrinkled hand, gently shaking the chess pieces. "Come on, stay awhile. Sit. I mean it—sit!"

Hamlet and I tried to sit in the pocket.

(Sitting in a pocket is trickier than it sounds.)

"Name's Ginger," she told Gus—or perhaps all of us—as

he somewhat reluctantly took his place at the table. "I always play white, so you're just going to have to deal with that. I'll try not to think of this as three against one." Ginger chuckled to herself, feather-coat fluttering.

I liked her!

(Nothing about Ginger reminded me of the lab.)

Hamlet concurred with a swift chomp of a tissue piece. Then we wiggled together, getting comfortable. *"Heeewhooooheeha,"* Gus said, wiggling, too. "Sorry, you're making me ticklish."

Ginger slapped a pawn into a middle square. "Don't know what I'm doing that's making you ticklish, son, but you should probably get that figured out. Take a trip to the doctor or something. Now, how long've you been playing the glorious game?"

Craning my head up, I could see Gus brightening. "Since I was four," he said. "But I'm staying with my grandpa right now—he's really good at chess, he was a professional before he quit—so I think I'm getting better. And I'm practicing with . . . someone else, too."

Someone else! That was me, Rosie!

My chin lifted proudly.

Which made Gus wiggle more.

"A seasoned talent," Ginger mused. "I like it. Now make your move. I'm eighty-six years old. I could die before we finish this game. Oh, don't look so shocked. I'm only toying with you!"

Slowly, Gus released a chuckle.

I settled in, observing the game: the way Gus advanced his pieces, the way Ginger navigated the board. *Move the rook! Stop, no! The rook!* Every once in a while, desire took hold of me. My paws pushed against the pocket. I wanted to be *inside* the game.

In six moves, Ginger had pinned Gus's king.

"Better luck next time," she said, winking one of her gray eyes. "Now you know how Marty felt."

Huh? Hamlet asked, as if he hadn't been paying attention at all. He started waving the tissue out of the pocket, like a little flag. The next person that Gus played was a man with a baseball cap who tapped his shoes to invisible music; his moves were precise, accurate. Like a machine in his brain was saying *Play this piece. Now this one. Now this.* Next up was a purple-dressed person. Then a yellow-dressed person. And then there was Mei.

"Wow," a girl said, approaching us. My ears perked at the sound of her sandals swishing against the grass. "Please don't take this the wrong way—because it's a good thing. But you smell *exactly* like Yeye. My grandfather." She sniffed, her whole face alight. "And also . . . raspberries?"

I wasn't afraid of the girl, either.

Not even a little.

Raspberries? Hamlet asked.

And Gus said, with a springy nod, "It's, um . . . jam! Thank you."

Whiskers fully awake and lifted in the pocket-y air, I studied the girl as she lowered herself into the seat across from us. Her fingers skipped over the pieces. She had a heart-shaped face, braided black hair, and ears as pink as Gus's. "I'm Mei. You're Gus?" she said, selecting a pawn. "I heard you talking to Ginger. Have you ever been here before? I haven't seen you. Normally I'm the youngest one. Not many kids want to wake up at seven in the morning to play chess. You got any pets?"

Hamlet inched up the pocket, curious.

I followed his lead.

"Um . . ." Gus said, trying to focus on his bishop. He readjusted his glasses, which were starting to fog in the humid summer air. "Not really? I mean, sort of. But no?"

"Oh." Mei bit her thumbnail, pensive. "I always thought I'd adopt a dog. Maybe like a beagle or something because they're *so* cute. With their floppy ears? And the way they howl. Sometimes when they bark, they get so into it, their front legs lift right off the ground."

Gus smiled. "I've seen that!"

"It's amazing, right? Your move. I just moved my queen. Anyway, my parents got me a cat—Purrito. My little brother named him. *I* wanted to call him Jiggles, but I was overruled. So, where do you go to school?"

As she spoke, I watched her facial expressions. Right before she made a devastating move, her lips quirked to the side. With a wiggle and a gentle kick to his chest, I tried to warn Gus about the impending checkmate.

But all he said was, *"Heeewhooooheeha."*

In the end, we won two games and lost three games. And with every player, I learned something new: something about strategy and human expressions and how to face an opponent. "Besides Ginger seeing you," Gus whispered into the pocket on the way back to his bike, "I think that went really well! Don't you?"

Well! Hamlet said, biting off another piece of the tissue.

"I don't know what you're saying!" Gus chirped, a bounce in his step. "But I think it's good! I think that—"

He jerked to a stop.

Next to my ear, I could hear his heartbeat triple.

Why? What's happening? What's—

"Don't. Move," Gus whispered. His voice didn't chirp anymore.

Then I glimpsed something that shivered my fur. Are you ready for it, Rosie?

There was an ice cream truck next to Gus's bike.

An ice cream truck, parked haphazardly on the grass, its jingling tune still ringing. Stepping from the driver's seat was . . .

I squinted, eyelids narrowing, trying to see.

Trying to make sure I was getting it right.

Gus gasped.

Because it was *him*, Rosie! The researcher who visited the house! The researcher, disguised as an ice cream man!

"Down," Gus said immediately, ducking behind the nearest trash can, and it was all Hamlet could do not to let out a ferocious, terrified squeak. And then sniff the trash. *Bananas!* (Actually, it *did* smell like there were bananas in there! My own nose lifted before I caught myself!)

Gus's chest rose and fell with each hard breath.

We waited, silent.

So quiet.

Until we heard a door slam, then the truck rumbling off in another direction. Gus peered over the trash can. "He's gone." Something cracked in his voice as he practically ran back to his bike. "I knew it. I *knew* there was something off about that ice cream truck. Remember when we saw it that night? With my binoculars! You don't think he saw me, do you? So he's just . . . scoping out the neighborhood? Like a surveillance thing? A secret surveillance thing, so no one knows it's the lab? And—oh my gosh!"

I popped my head fully out of the pocket, then saw them, too. Stapled to a tree, right next to Gus's bike, was a series of WANTED posters.

Me!

I was on the posters!

Me, in the lab, staring straight into the camera. Eyes circular. Tail straight. Beneath my toes, block letters spelled: WANTED, PREFERABLY ALIVE TO MAINTAIN SPECIMEN, SUBJECT 7 KNOWN AS "WONDERMOUSE." IF FOUND, PLEASE CALL NUMBER BELOW IMMEDIATELY. LARGE REWARD.

"Big mistake!" Gus yelped, hurrying away from the posters. "Coming here was a big, big, *big* mistake!"

Straddling the bike, he didn't stop to put us in the basket.

We just took off, hearts trembling, checking over our shoulders for the ice cream truck.

We just sped back to Pop's house. Light chased us through the trees.

It wasn't until later that we realized that someone had followed us home.

Always,

Clementine

Letter 23

Dear Rosie,

We exploded into the house. Hamlet and I were holding each other in Gus's pocket, and Pop bolted from the kitchen. "Oh, thank goodness," he said, rushing toward us. "I was spinning myself into a ball of yarn, worrying about the three of you! I thought I'd go search, but I wasn't certain where to look. All of these scenarios rushed through my mind! Kidnapped by the lab! Kidnapped by—"

"Pop!" Gus said, extracting us gently from the pocket. I clung to his wrist, visions of the researcher still glowing in my brain. "It *was* the lab. The ice cream truck! The *ice cream truck*!"

Pop paused, beard puffed like a cloud of flour. "I'm going to need more information."

So, balancing on Gus's wrist, I mimed what we saw, using my paws. *The researcher! The park! Ice cream!* I was very thorough.

"Nope," Pop said, "still need more."

"Someone from the lab's surveilling the neighborhood!" Gus burst out. He said it so loudly, his glasses wobbled. "In an old ice cream truck! I should've left a note. Or tried harder to wake you up. Or not have left at all. I just got so worried about them. About both of them—Hamlet and Clementine—and all the other mice in the lab. What if they're already smart? Really smart? And they're showing signs that they're different? What'll the lab do to them? So I panicked and found this chess club that meets at the park and . . . I should've waited. But I didn't think I had time to wait. But that was *such* a bad thing to do." He paused, realization floating across his face. "My dad's right about me, isn't he? I *am* a bad kid. Stupid, stupid, *stupid*—"

Gus! I squeaked, clambering up to his shoulder. I tugged his earlobe. Once. Twice. Tug, tug. Because he wasn't stupid. Or bad. He was a human trying the best he could.

Pop quickly shuffled over and placed a hand on Gus's empty shoulder. "What? What are you talking about, my Gus? Listen to me. You have the biggest heart. The *biggest* heart. And it scares me when you put yourself in danger, because I love you more than my life. Do you understand? We will absolutely come back to this, but right now, I need to know what you saw. Exactly what you saw. How did you learn about this truck?"

My eyes widened, once more, at the memory.

Gus blinked frantically. "The posters! One of the researchers—the same guy who came to your house! When Clementine turned on the blender and stuff! He was hanging up these posters at the park. Posters with Clementine's face on them! And—"

At this point, someone knocked on the door.

The noise jolted through us.

We were followed!

I squeaked again, directly into Gus's ear, and I could hear Hamlet, still shivering in Gus's hand. He was squealing, too. Calling out for me.

Was this the end? Was it? Was it, Rosie?

"This is all my fault!" Gus shout-whispered. "I'm so sorry, Clementine!"

Apples? I thought, springing from his shoulder, frantically trying to wedge myself into the fruit bowl. *Bananas? Bananas? Could I hide behind bananas? Hamlet! Here!*

The knock sounded again.

"I led the researchers right to us." Gus was still whispering, tears forming in the corners of his eyes. "They thought something was fishy before, and now they know, and— Maybe we could ignore them? We don't have to open the door!"

The doorbell rang now.

Over and over.

When I popped my head through the fruit, gazing back to Pop, I saw that he was breathing deeply through his nostrils. "Clementine can hide with the feather dusters," he said, voice tempered. "In the living room, by the bookshelf. Leave it to me to handle our visitor . . . Just please, Gus, whatever you do, refrain from putting the mice in your shirt! Or anywhere near your trousers."

"I . . . I can do that," Gus said.

So he placed me and Hamlet in the feather dusters, the fibers poking our bellies. *Oooh! Ha! That tickles.*

Pop flew out of the room, white hair puffing behind him. His gardening boots (and the rest of him!) thumped toward the *ding-ding-dong* of the bell. Over the pitter-patter of my heart, over the sharp creaking of the door, I heard him mumble, "Everything will be fine. Fine, fine . . . Marty?"

Fine, fine, Hamlet repeated, head bobbing, as if it were a song.

You will not believe what happened next. Or maybe you *will* believe what happened next. Because I've just told you. It was Marty at the door. And Mei. And Ginger.

Should I still be afraid? Or relieved? Or both?

"Marty indeed!" said Ginger, stepping into the foyer. Her cane clacked against the hardwood. (*Oh! Oh!* I thought, whiskers deep in feathers. *These dusters match her coat.*) "Showed up just in time for me to wipe the floor with him, yet again. You two know each other? Small town, I guess. I don't suppose you have any lemonade?"

"I like lemonade," Mei said, smiling.

Pop stepped back, now perfectly calm. "Well, you were not who I was expecting."

"Let's cut to the chase!" Ginger bellowed. Everyone followed her across the plush rug, and she tapped her cane twice on the rug for extra attention. "Your young friend here? Bus?"

"Gus," Gus said, gently correcting her.

"Gus," Ginger said, snapping her teeth to emphasize the word. "Gus might not be a ringer, but he *did* show up today with those mice from the news."

"They're not—" Gus began.

"Save it," Ginger said. "I'm eighty-six. The news is my life. I know all about Wondermouse and her runaway friend. And so do the rest of us."

The group murmured and nodded.

Which terrified and pleased me. I couldn't decide whether to retreat farther into the feathers, or burst from the bookshelf, offering a *Hello! Hello! Hi! It's me.*

"I just wanted some time," Ginger said, brushing a strand of her blue hair from her forehead, "to figure out what we were going to do about it. And this is what we're going to do about it . . ."

Everyone waited.

My tail curled in hesitation.

"What are you *waiting* for?" she bellowed again. "I said *this* is what we're going to do about it. *This.* Right here, right now. We all discussed it after you left, quorum style, and decided that we'd be a bunch of nincompoops if we didn't decide to help. Whatever we can do to save them, we'll do it. Now, my guess is we don't have a moment to waste, so spit it out, Bus. What's our next move?"

Gus looked at Pop in disbelief.

And then both of them started beaming.

You see, Rosie? You see?

Some humans pick me up by the tail.

But some humans are good.

Always,

Clementine

Letter 24

Dear Rosie,

I told everyone *welcome*, launching myself from the dusters. *Welcome to you! And to you!* Toes tingling, I settled on the laces of Gus's sneakers. "I found them in the *mailbox*," he was explaining, hands animated and wild. "One of them was clutching a whisker. Then he fainted! I didn't know CPR, and . . ." He told Ginger about the researcher, and our chess training, and how I'd play a game against Agnes live on television—proving that I was worthy of saving.

"That's the wildest idea I've ever heard," said Ginger, smiling with all her teeth. "But doggone it, don't the wild ones always work?"

"Ahhh! Ah!" shrieked Marty, who was lingering near the back. He was around Pop's age and wore a green felt cap—and a mouse on his shoulder. (It was Hamlet! Hamlet had crawled up his plaid jacket for a better view.)

Good idea! I climbed onto Ginger's shoulder, nestling in the feathers. My paws kneaded the fabric.

"Ahoy!" she said to me. "I feel like a true pirate now. Better a mouse than a toucan on my shoulder. What're those birds called? Toucans? Parrots? Oh, never mind. What were you saying, young man?"

"Clementine really needs some new opponents," Gus enthused, so excited I could feel his energy halfway across the room. "This morning was great, but she could play against you herself!"

"Then, you!" Ginger said, pointing at Pop with her cane. I rocked back a little in the feathers as she advanced forward. *Little step. Little step. Rock.* "I'm assuming you've got more than one chessboard? Chop, chop! You said we only have three more days?" She sucked air through her rather large teeth. "Not that much time, but we'll work with what we've got. Onward, Marty!"

Pop hurried to fulfill Ginger's request, grabbing all the chessboards in the house—the plastic ones and the wood ones, the classic and the themed. "The medieval set," Pop declared, plunking it on the couch. He'd tidied his hair a little, so it rested gracefully at his shoulders. "The knights have meticulous suits of armor. And, let's see, the animal set: lions for the kings, bear cubs and little chimpanzees for the pawns . . . And finally! The Alice in Wonderland set."

Little chimpanzees?

I was still stuck on *little chimpanzees*.

Balancing on Ginger's shoulder, I wobbled onto my hind legs, front paws clasped together. *Rosie. Rosie, are those pieces shaped like you?*

"All these newfangled things," said Ginger, examining the boxes. She seemed to enjoy the fanfare. I hung on to the feathers as she bent over. "What're you doing up there, mouse? Ah, I don't like the shoulder feathers, either. Should've gone with the glitter gemstones. Rip 'em up, if you'd like! Now, Mei, you play at the dining table. Marty, take the coffee table. Everyone else, spread out. Everyone except you, Gus. Or is it Bus? Anyway, you stick with me. There's a special job for you."

Pop scrunched his enormous frame into the corner of the couch, the animal set on his lap. "Are we playing a simultaneous?" he asked, enormous eyebrows arching. "Is that what's occurring?"

"Absolutely." Ginger grinned. "She's going to play all of us at once."

At once? Back toes gripping the feathers, I brought my front paws together again. In shock. In thought. The idea . . . excited me.

"We're going to throw the kitchen sink at you, mouse," Ginger said, "and see what sticks. I'm mixing my metaphors here, but never mind. Onward, troops!"

We began!

The four humans played white, moving first.

The sound of pawns advanced around the house. It tickled my ears.

And Gus plucked me from Ginger's shoulder, carrying me from board to board, from player to player.

"Aren't you afraid she's going to poop on you?" Marty said, pointing to me in Gus's hand. Like a habit, he adjusted the rim of his felt hat. "I had a hamster once. Geronimo. He pooped *everywhere*."

"Um," Gus said, adjusting his glasses. "No, I think she's good."

Carefully, against Marty, I stretched my paws out— then played my knight.

Against Pop, I started the Sicilian Defense, my toes tingling with giddiness. "Ah," he said, smoothing the tips of his mustache. His eyes glowed with pride. "Very smart, Clementine."

Then there was Mei. And Ginger. Keeping track of four games should've been difficult. Remembering my strategies and the board positioning should've been tricky. But here's the thing, Rosie.

My brain glowed.

My brain thrived in this environment.

The maze was expanding all around me—and yet! And

yet I could see my way past the twists and turns, right to the very end.

"Faster, little mouse!" Ginger said. "Faster!"

So I made my moves faster—thinking quicker, shifting the pieces quicker. Hamlet had found his way to Mei. Every time I visited her board, he was inching closer to her fingers. Asking, maybe, for her to smooth the fur of his head. (Yes, that was it. I've never heard a mouse purr before! He purred!)

Anyway!

I pinned Marty's king in six moves.

"Oh," he said, reclining in the armchair and clucking his tongue. He tossed his felt hat on the table. "That's a shame. A wonderful shame. Who would've thought it? Beaten by a mouse! You're a real whippersnapper. I hope you give Ginger a run for her money!"

Ginger lost in seven.

She threw her head back and laughed. At which point, my head dipped and tilted. I could see her teeth glitter from below! "I knew you'd excel in a simultaneous!" Ginger exclaimed, tapping her wrists. "I just knew it! Ha! These old bones never lie. They once predicted a snowstorm in the middle of August! That's a true story, Marty. Marty, stop laughing or I'll come over there."

Mei held on for five more moves before tipping over

her king. "I surrender," she said, grinning. One of her front teeth was crossed over the other, like Gus's, and it winked in the light. "Normally I hate losing, but . . . it feels different this time."

Now there was only Pop left.

"You're doing *exceptional*, little mouse," he said. In the middle of the board, I craned my neck up—catching his expression. Which was hopeful. And pleased. He didn't even seem to notice the entire sprig of parsley lost in the hair behind his ear. "Truly, truly exceptional."

He slid his knight.

I pushed a pawn.

A pawn shaped exactly like a chimpanzee.

When it was my turn again, one of my paws reached out to stroke the wood—all the smoothly carved lines, the ridges of raised fur. So small. You were my size! What were you doing, at that exact moment?

What are you doing now?

Are you missing me?

Are you safe?

I liked having you on the board. But you shouldn't have been a pawn. You should've been a queen.

"Clementine?"

Pop's voice cut through my thoughts.

Yes? My head whipped around.

"Little mouse," he crooned. "You've been staring at that pawn for six minutes straight."

I noticed, with a tiny shock, that the other humans had circled around us. Mei, who was rather smitten with Hamlet, had cupped him in her hands. Ginger had bent over, a few inches from the board, examining our strategies with big gray eyes. Gus peered at me openly, twiddling his thumbs with concern.

Six minutes?

Six minutes had passed?

"You had me worried," Pop said, one giant hand over his heart. "But there's no rush. No rush. Whenever you're ready . . ."

So I slid my bishop across the board, feeling its heavy weight.

Rosie, why is everything so much heavier than before?

"Mmm." Pop brought a finger to his lips and surveyed the board. "Mmmm. That's . . . Mmmm. That's quite the move. Incredibly imaginative. In return, I'll play my . . ." He hesitated, smiling. His eyes flicked from his king to my knight. "I think you've given me no choice. It seems that I'm about to be on the run."

He pushed his king a space to the left.

Which gave me an opening. A chance.

With one final sweep, my tail trailing behind me, I

moved my queen out from behind the bishop, delivering the checkmate.

Pop's eyes twinkled as the other humans clapped. "Yes, little mouse," he said, his voice watery with pride. "Very good. Very good indeed. I've played all sorts of humans in my life, but have never had an opponent quite like you. And I don't mean the fact that you're a mouse. I mean"—he tapped his forehead—"I mean *up here*. The way your minds works. It's astounding. You are unlike anyone. Surely that's enough to keep you safe."

I tried, very hard, to believe him.

Always,

Clementine

Letter 25

Dear Rosie,

Have you ever heard of Stuart Little? Or *Ratatouille*? I had so many questions, there in the living room, as Gus and Mei spoke. Should I assume my listening position, forepaws tucked under my chin? They'd been talking for almost four minutes! Four long minutes!

"This is *just* like Stuart Little," Mei repeated, dragging her knees to her chest. She'd stayed behind while the others had left, Ginger and Marty promising to return tomorrow. I'd lost my game with Pop—but maybe, in the morning, I'd have better luck. "Except for the fact that he could talk like a human. And he wasn't a lab mouse." She shuddered. "And he got stuck in the washing machine."

The way she said it made me believe that I would not like to be stuck in a washing machine.

"Oh, don't worry, Clementine," she told me, her eyes earnest. Her black braids swung gently over her shoulders. "That won't happen to you."

"Mice have really bad luck in books," Gus added. "People keep trying to get rid of them." He peered down at me sheepishly. "I guess that's kind of true in real life, too. There's this book about witches . . ."

"*The Witches*!" Mei said, clapping her hands. "I was just thinking about that. I *loved* that book. But . . ." She shuddered again, her cat-ear headband shivering. "They did turn those kids into mice so they could exterminate them."

Now it was Hamlet's turn to tremble. Or was he just shaking his fur?

Either way, *exterminate* is a tail-trembling word.

"Terrible things can happen to mice all the time," Mei said sadly. "You have to admit, though, this whole thing is pretty cool. I've never had so much fun playing chess! My yeye taught me mah-jongg last summer, and I got obsessed with it. Like, *obsessed*. But Yeye lives in Ohio and there's nowhere to play mah-jongg around here. Chess was the best I could come up with."

Gus cleared his throat. "I could learn mah-jongg, if you want. We could play together the next time I visit."

"Really?" Mei brightened. "It's really complicated. Are you sure?"

Gus nodded enthusiastically, and I did, too. It sounded like a very good idea!

"That's . . . wow," Mei said. "Thanks! Now, can I try something? Do you have a calculator, Gus? I've been wanting to give this a shot for hours." Gus fished out a long plastic calculator from a nearby drawer, and Mei pressed several buttons. "Can you do math and stuff, Clementine? What's four thousand three hundred and twelve times five thousand six hundred and one?"

She cleared the answer, then laid the calculator by my feet.

"Calculate it in your mind," she told me, "and then tap the numbers."

"Even if she can't solve this," Gus said, "there are all kinds of intelligences, I think. Geniuses come in all shapes and sizes, and—"

24151512

As he was speaking, I had already punched in the numbers.

"Whoa!" Gus said. "Is that right?"

"I can't really remember," Mei said, laughing. "But yeah, I think so!"

Then they started giggling together, as Hamlet waddled over to try his own paw at the calculator.

77.34, he typed, then divided it by 100.

"0.7734," Gus read. "Okay. He's just testing out some numbers?"

"No," Mei said emphatically, turning the calculator upside down. "See how it reads now? When you flip it over? It spells *HELLO*."

Hello, Hamlet concurred with a nod.

It gave me an idea.

Always,
Clementine

Letter 26

Dear Rosie,

That night, I thought about you, Rosie. How would you play chess? You'd probably examine each move with stolen pieces in your mouth. When you'd smile, they'd all be there: the bishops sticking out like extra teeth. (Hilarious! You always know how to make me laugh.)

In the terrarium, I kept remembering the chimpanzee pawns, the ones shaped like you. They were too heavy for me to carry upstairs. After Mei left, my front paws pointed to them—over and over—but Gus didn't fully comprehend. "I . . . I like that board, too," he said.

Hours later, Hamlet was mirroring me as I paced. I sidestepped, he sidestepped. I tail-twirled, he tail-twirled. I decided that now was a good time to head downstairs. Scrambling up the nearest succulent, working together to roll up the mesh topper, we hooked ourselves over the ledge. Paws dragging, our bellies *squuueeaaakk*ed against the glass as we dropped.

Banister? Hamlet's eyes pleaded at the top of the stairs. *We slide down the banister?*

Danger! I said.

Danger-fun! he said, shimmying up the wall's rough surface. Should he slide down on his back, tail akimbo? Should he stick all four legs in the air and glide? Or maybe a belly-down approach would do? I'm not in Hamlet's mind, Rosie. I don't know whether he dreams in Latin, whether he ponders earth's gravitational force as he chews a green bean. But I do know he asked these questions. They were written all over his wide, hopeful face.

Belly-up it was.

Weeeeeeeeee! he said in our mouse language.

Hamlet! I said.

At the bottom of the banister, he couldn't figure out how to stop—catapulting himself into the air, legs flailing, launching into the soil of a houseplant. He emerged, whiskers dyed black, shaking dirt from his ears. I checked to see if he was all right. If he was still in one piece.

He was!

I am! he said, following me to the animal kingdom chessboard. *What are we doing!*

Chess! I said.

Me?

You!

173

Wasn't it the best way to help myself? Wasn't it the best way to help all of us, Rosie? While Gus and Pop were sleeping, Hamlet and I could practice. I'd like to believe that I can help us, outside of the humans. Just me. Just a lab mouse.

Or, rather, *two* lab mice.

If he can type *HELLO* into a calculator, on his own accord, then surely he can play chess?

Hamlet knocked the rook with his tail. It rocked before toppling over, sending him scurrying. He peered back at the board from a hole in a throw pillow, stuffing under his chin—exactly like Pop's beard.

It's okay! I told him with my own tail. *They won't hurt you!*

The words tumbled between my ears. *They won't hurt you. They won't hurt you.* Almost as if I were remembering something. Why was Hamlet so afraid?

Gently, I coaxed him back.

Gently, I taught him the rules.

At first, chess didn't seem to interest him. So many pieces! So many strategies! White, black, bishop, king, Queen's Gambit, King's Gambit, Sicilian Defense. Swap your rook here, avoid that trap, push the pawns like so. It took him sixteen minutes. Then his eyes began to spark. *Oh! Oh! OH! Like maze.*

174

Like the maze, I repeated. *Yet better*.

He has an interesting style, Rosie. Interesting quirks. Before each move, he places both paws on his back and stretches in a deep arch. He massages his whiskers, letting out a soft *chutter-chutter* sound. He moves the pieces like he's dancing, kicking his back legs high in the air. To a beat, almost! Cha-cha-CHA! Cha-cha-CHA!

And he sacrifices more pieces than any player I know.

A bishop for a knight.

A pawn for a rook.

Always this for that—to advance himself across the board. In our fifth game, he even traded his queen. He just let her go! Also, he almost won. He almost won *because* of that move—because he'd given himself a path to the other side.

I guess if anyone knows sacrifice, it's a lab mouse.

Rosie?

I'm looking up at you now. Not the real you. The chess you. The one with carved ears and carved eyes. The smile is halfway the same. With one trembling paw, I reach out, out—to feel the ridges. Of your shoulders. Of your nose.

Huh, Hamlet says, sidling up to me.

Hello.

Huh-OHM, he responds.

My ears tilt up.

Hohm, he says again. Then a final: *Home.*

With his tail, he gestures back and forth between me and the chimpanzee. Between me and you. *Home, home, home.*

My heart floats. He knows? He knows! Did Hamlet see me sneaking into your cage at night? Did he ever follow me? Or . . .

Just as quickly, my heart plummets. My belly sinks.

Or . . . he has a Rosie, too.

Many Rosies, I realize, as I notice how wide his eyes are. How sad his eyes are. Many Rosies. All the mice he played with. All the mice he cuddled with. All the mice he left behind.

So I clean him. I clean him with my paws, smoothing the fur on his back. I wash behind his ears and between the pads of his toes. Isn't this what mice do?

Thank you, he says, closing his eyes. *Thank you thank you home.*

Always,
Clementine

Letter 27

Dear Rosie,

Am I upsetting you? Was the last letter too sad? When I remember this part, when I think about the words I've written, I'll try to tell you in an upbeat way. I'll try to keep the spirit of the moment—but let you know that everything turned out okay. That everything *is* okay.

Because someday, somehow, I still believe that we might meet again.

And Hamlet! You might meet Hamlet.

You can teach him how to spell. And how to *hoot*. And how a chimpanzee can cup a mouse in the palm of her hand. Sometimes, when I drift off—allowing my eyes to close—you're there, holding me. Cradling me. You will forever be the best thing at the end of the maze.

"Breakfast!" Pop said eagerly, his voice floating in from the hallway. "Should we mix it up today, my Gus? Wait a moment. I think I left my lucky tea mug right in here. I wonder if Clementine . . . Clementine!"

"Clementine?" Gus parroted, pausing before the chessboard where Hamlet and I were taking a thirty-second break from play. When he spotted us, his eyes bulged behind his glasses. "You guys! I thought you were still in the terrarium!" He cocked his head, two tufts of hair sticking up. "Wait, you *were* in the terrarium. I saw you!"

Well. Yes!

Before we departed, Hamlet and I nibbled the whitish stuffing from Gus's pillow, then rolled the fluff in soil; we molded it to look like ourselves. One Clementine-shaped lump. One Hamlet-shaped lump. Both together, in the hammock. Otherwise, wouldn't Gus wake up and worry?

Had we upset him now? Nervously, Hamlet and I wrung our tails with our paws. (I guess, now that we've fully bonded, I'm mirroring him, too.)

Gus scratched behind one of his ears, as if he were still trying to piece together the puzzle. "At least you're not kidnapped or anything. You're safe."

Safe for now, my brain said. This morning, Rosie, it was as if I could *feel* time ticking. As if my brain were a clock, counting down the seconds in the broadcast. And there wasn't a single second to waste!

Now that I was in charge of my own training, I didn't hesitate. I just kept practicing. Gus took over for Hamlet, settling next to me in his wrinkled pajamas; he looked more confident after yesterday. Was I imagining it, Rosie? He sat up a bit straighter. Paused before moving his pieces.

Pop looked lighter, too. "This calls for *kagianas*," he said, clapping his hands. "Scrambled eggs, tomatoes, feta. Eggs keep your mind very sharp. We can't play chess on empty stomachs, can we?"

No, I thought, remembering the juice from the greenhouse tomatoes—and how well I'd played later that day. *Food is always a good choice!*

After we'd eaten, my paws flitted between letters in the alphabet book.

M-E-I.

Mei. We need Mei for practicing, too.

So she arrived—along with Ginger and Marty. Marty brought bagels (with seeds! tiny seeds!) and taught me how to use a chess clock: by jumping on top of the stopper between moves. (I jumped. Marty did not jump! I wanted to make that clear.) For her part, Ginger taught me the eagle-eye stare.

"It's just like a bear's," she said, "if that bear was *crossed* with an eagle. I'm going to do it for three seconds and three seconds only, because I'm not sure you can handle any more than that. You whip this out when you're trying to confuse your opponent. Ready?"

Her pupils hardened. She narrowed the whites of her eyes.

Oh! I see it!

My paws traveled to my own eyes to block the view.

"Now, you be careful with that," she added, tapping her cane twice for emphasis. "It's a weapon you might never have to use. With great power comes great responsibility."

A little later, Mei shared a new chess opening. "It's called the Frankenstein-Dracula Variation," she said, braiding a few strands of her black hair. I held my paws to my chin as I peered up at her. "That's its real name! I found it online last night. I thought you should have some little-known openings in your pocket if you want to try and stump a speed-chess player like Agnes. There's also the Hippopotamus Defense and the Toilet Variation." Mei wrinkled her nose. "The last one doesn't sound too good, but—"

"The lab," Pop said suddenly. Ominously. His eyes, usually so sharp, had a hint of mist in the corners. A hint of fear. In one of his hands, a phone glistened.

The lab what?

My heartbeat quickened. Next to me, Hamlet clutched a rook for comfort.

Everyone in the room had spun to look at Pop. Chatter stilled. Ears perked.

"It could be ... not good," he said slowly, moving toward the television. His boots, still mismatched, squeaked the whole way there. "My producer just rang, down at the station. I had a long conversation with her yesterday about animals in labs, because I was trying to work through my speech for the show. She called and mentioned ... Well, she mentioned this. There's a special broadcast starting in a minute or two."

Gus inched closer toward me, his hand protectively at my back. I let myself settle onto his knee, which was bouncing. Nervously. Jiggling me. "Do they know?" Gus asked, face turning white. His voice became increasingly frantic. "They don't . . . they don't know she's here, do they? They don't know about the other mice? Pop, what if they know about the other mice?"

Pop's pockets drooped. Like all the air had deflated inside them. He'd paused by the TV, his hand on the remote control—as if he wasn't sure that he wanted to push the button. "I don't know, my Gus. Clementine, I . . ." He trailed off, words lost in his mustache. "Be brave."

What's happening?

What is it?

I'm a small mouse, so I notice small things. Right then, I noticed the way Pop's eyes clouded. How Ginger clutched her cane a bit tighter. How Mei tugged on the bottom of her braid.

I believe that our story will end well.

So . . . why doesn't it feel that way right now?

Always,
Clementine

Letter 28

Dear Rosie,

You're always here. Hence the sign-off for my letters. I may be gone from you, but you are always knuckle-walking at the front of my mind. And now . . . now! The TV burst to life, colors and shapes and sounds filtering into the room. My brain scurried everywhere at once. Because it was you, Rosie. On the TV.

It was *you*.

"Are they trying to convince the public that their experiments are ethical?" Pop asked, fingers in his beard. Grimly, his eyes flitted over the scene. "I suppose the chimpanzee is to show the welfare of the animals . . . but my word! Anyone can see she's afraid."

"Welfare," Ginger harrumphed. "She's miserable! Look at her! Look at her face."

"Poor chimp," Mei whispered.

And I thought, *Rosie.*

Rosie.

Rosie.

You were in the parking lot of the lab. A researcher held you in his arms, and you were gripping his back with your fingers. Faster than I've ever scampered, I catapulted myself from Gus's knee, swooped up to the TV stand—and climbed. Climbing. Climbing, reaching toward the screen, until your face was hovering above me. Static clung to my toes as I pressed my paws to the TV.

I'm here. It's me. I'm here.

"See?" a researcher said. He patted your head. "As we've claimed all along, our animals receive the best care possible. They're an integral part of scientific progress. The history of medicine *is* the history of animal testing. We respect that some people might feel differently, but look at this one. Does she look unhappy?"

Yes. Unhappy.

You looked so different, Rosie. Because I left? Or did I not notice before? When you peered at the camera, chimp teeth flashing, your black coat didn't shimmer. Your amber eyes were duller. Flatter. My reflection wilted inside them.

"Same goes for the mice," the researcher said—the one with the crooked eyebrows. Another one who used to pick me up by the tail. "Each of our mice is treated with care."

"Until you want to kill them!" Gus exploded.

Nose smushed against the TV screen, I thought: *In the background, is that . . . ? Felix!* Felix, sweating through his lab coat. Beads slipped down his forehead. His hair glowed orange in the morning light.

"We're also following several new leads," the tail-picking researcher said, "and are narrowing down three or four possible locations for the stolen mice. That's all. No questions."

A few reporters shouted after him.

Then you were gone.

Rosie, you're gone. No more chimp ears on the TV screen. No more chimp palms, outstretched toward the sun. So quick, so quick. Did you have time to feel the sky?

Always,

Clementine

Letter 29

Dear Rosie,

The first time I saw a letter, it was pinned above Felix's desk. *Dear Felix*, the handwriting said. *We're getting lots of sun here in Tahiti.*

In these letters, Rosie, should I have noted the weather? The changing colors of the sky? It didn't seem fair, if your sky never changes, if your cage never sees the sun. Is that what you were doing, all those times? Some nights, I'd round the corner, and I'd catch you—eyes on the metal ceiling. Like you were staring through it. Like you were searching for the light.

And I'd sit there with you, eyes up.

I never knew what we were looking at. But if you were staring, I knew there was something to be seen.

Rosie, were you an Outside Chimpanzee once?

Did you have a family?

Were there other chimpanzees who looked exactly like you? Who had your soft face, your amber eyes? Were there trees in your old world? Leafy trees with swinging branches, and low-hanging fruit that you could eat whenever you wanted?

I told you about the electric warmth of those lamps— how I knew they weren't really light. I understood by instinct. I think you know by sight, by touch, by the loss of it.

Rosie, if you dream, I hope that sunflowers are still growing inside you.

Always,

Clementine

Letter 30

Dear Rosie,

What now? My body is sluggish. My toes aren't working right. *Tap. Tap.* I'm still tapping them on the TV screen; I can't seem to pull myself away.

"Clementine?" Gus asks, leaving the couch. He shuffles up behind me, until his shadow is my shadow, too. "Clementine . . . you know that chimpanzee, don't you?"

"She does, all right," says Ginger, without a second of hesitation. Her voice has an odd tone to it, like she's speaking through woodchips. "Just look at her. Those whiskers? Looks like me after my friend Ethel went away."

Away.

Isn't it interesting how some of the biggest words have the fewest syllables? *Home. Gone. Away. Pneumonoultramicroscopicsilicovolcanoconiosis*, for example, is longer, but it doesn't make you feel the same.

And I'm feeling . . .

Everything.

I slowly turn around to face Gus and let myself crawl into his waiting palm. Wallowing in the warmth there. The comfort there.

It's not enough.

Mei shudders, goose bumps on her arms. "I didn't even know they used chimpanzees in labs. And dogs? Did you hear those dogs howling in the background?"

Hamlet perches on Mei's knee, front toes tightly knit with worry. Overwhelmed, all I can do is catch his eye and stare back at him, unblinking. *She looked thin, Hamlet? She looked sad?*

Home, he replies, his eyes like black beads in the light. He appears more concerned than I've ever seen him. *Huh-ohm.*

Rosie?

Rosie, I've tried to be a good lab mouse. A good lab mouse who does her best for science. But when have the researchers ever done their best for *us*?

I will do my best for you. And for Hamlet. And for the other mice, still trapped in the lab. Maybe if I play chess well—no, if I play *extraordinarily*—the message will be big enough for all of us. Won't humans understand? Won't humans see?

If a mouse can win a chess game, then a chimpanzee should have a blanket. A chimpanzee should eat fresh fruit every morning. A chimpanzee should never be that thin.

"She's thinking," Gus says, sadness in his words. "She's got her thinking face on. And she smells like raspberries."

Yes, something's coming. Something's brewing and blinking and thickening, my brain aglow. Suddenly, my ears whip back! My tail sticks straight out! Because I've got it.

Our game needs to be bigger.

Bigger!

Flinging out my legs, I parachute from Gus's hand, landing with a *thump* on my feet. The book? Where's the book? Where's the—*oh!* By the soil pots, tucked by the fireplace. Gus realizes what I'm looking for, picks up the book, and opens to the first alphabet page.

"*S*," he says as I skitter. "*I-M-U* . . ."

Legs! Must! Work! Faster!

I urge myself on, jumping high on each letter, so eager to share my idea.

"Simultaneous," Gus finally says. "You want to play a simultaneous . . . on TV?"

My entire body nods vigorously.

"That's . . ." Pop says, voice floating across the room. "That's a brilliant idea, Clementine. Yes!" His enormous eyebrows fluff together as he thinks. "You could certainly raise the impact that way. You'd be . . . Well, you'd be undeniable! A mouse playing a *single* person is one thing. But a mouse playing three people? Or four? Or five? You can play Agnes—and you can also play all of us."

"I'm in," Ginger says, rising slowly to her feet. Her cane wobbles before she steadies herself, chest puffed. "After the game, anyone who wants to take her, they'll have to get through *me* first. They don't call me Ginger 'The Fist' Sutherbee for nothing."

Marty takes off his felt hat and tosses it to the side, standing with Ginger. "No one calls you that, Ginger. But, doggone it, I guess I'm in, too."

Mei bolts from her chair to go stand alongside them. "And me! I'll do it. If that's what Clementine wants."

Beneath the sadness, my heart is swelling so much, beating so much.

Everyone is on their feet.

For us, Rosie.

For us.

Always,

Clementine

Letter 31

Dear Rosie,

It's day five of my escape. Tomorrow is day six! Tomorrow, I'll take my place in front of the television cameras. The mouse in me is everywhere. Mind, everywhere! Thinking about the broadcast, the importance of the broadcast, what will happen if I fail, what will happen if the audience doesn't understand what we're trying to accomplish.

Rosie? Will you forgive me?

I'm still very optimistic, but will you forgive me if no one sees? If no one sees that we're worthy? My original goal was to stay alive. But now, it's about showing that we all deserve better—mice *and* chimpanzees.

The chess club comes over again, and I practice until my front legs are sore. Until my mind is gluey. During a round of speed chess, I start to lose in the middle game. Lose against Ginger. Lose against Pop. He stops the clock and places a finger on my shoulder. "You're getting inside your head, Clementine. Usually that's a good place to be . . . but this is not you. This is not how you play. Don't let the stress consume you."

Pulling myself together, I tighten my endgame and win—but *everyone* is becoming increasingly stressed. Mei is biting her fingernails. Marty is chattering nonsensically about his great-great-aunt Matilda's cats. And Gus tells Pop, in the kitchen: "I'm starting to get a bad feeling in my stomach."

Me, too! I wobble on the countertop, brussels sprout clutched between my paws. A brussels sprout, finally.

It's chewy. It's green. It's delicious.

And yet . . . not even vegetables can quell the feeling. The rising feeling. The feeling that, no matter how optimistic I am, this might not turn out all right after all. I am a mouse after all. A mouse who is just trying her best.

"See you bright and early," Ginger squawks as night descends on Pop's garden. With her pinkie finger, she bonks me lightly between my ears. "Now I'm going to get my beauty sleep. Clementine? You get your brain sleep. We're gonna give 'em heck tomorrow. You can bet your life on it. Okay! Marty, all right. That was a poor turn of phrase. You can bet your . . . tail on it? Too aggressive. Never mind! Good night, good night—goodbye."

Mei gives me an extra-soft pat as they leave.

And immediately, Gus, Pop, Hamlet, and I sweep upstairs. Way upstairs. Up a rickety ladder, into the attic. An attic, it occurs to me, is the perfect place for mice! Lots of nooks and crannies. Lots of secret spaces. Plus, cardboard boxes! Plenty of chewable cardboard.

"I know I have it *somewhere*," Pop says, tossing clothes over his shoulder, sweaters flying from boxes. He reminds me of Hamlet with the sunflower seeds. "I've kept dozens of costumes over the years . . ." Finally, he extracts a short, cream-colored stretch of fabric, holding it up in the dim attic light.

Gus gulps. I'm in his palm. So it's like I can feel the gulping. "Are you sure I should wear a tie?"

"Well, I told your father about your impending TV appearance . . ."

Gus's ears sink in the dim attic light. "And what'd he say?"

"That you should wear a tie," Pop says, cocking his head at the dangling piece of fabric. "But now that I'm witnessing it myself, I'm convinced that's a terrible idea. Wear whatever you feel most comfortable in." He pauses, hands on his hips. "The mood in this room is downright gloomy."

It's true. My whiskers are limp.

In the terrarium by Gus's feet, Hamlet joins in the gloom.

Pop drops the tie back in the cardboard box, stepping
toward us in his boots. The attic floor creaks. "What would
you say, Clementine, to a late-night dinner on the roof?"

The roof?

"The roof?" Gus asks, brightening a little. I brighten
along with his brightening. "Are we allowed to do that?"

"Besides the general laws of physics, I shouldn't see
why not." Pop knocks on the wood above his head, rap-
ping with all his knuckles. "There's a flat bit here. Just takes
some maneuvering. And we're under the cover of darkness now. Clementine, on your last night, you deserve to
see the stars. Shall I rustle us up some asparagus?"

No one should say no to asparagus, Rosie.

That is a rule for living.

In the kitchen, Gus washes a bushel of tomatoes,
Hamlet batting the water with his paws (then frantically
wiping his face, trying to get the water *off, off, off*), and Pop
chops the ends off asparagus, adding more vegetables to
a basket with strawberries and arugula and apples and—

"You think that's enough?" Gus asks.

"Let's see," Pop says, a smile beneath his mustache.
"With careful estimation, I believe we could feed about
six hundred mice. So yes. That'll do."

We climb.

We climb another ladder onto the flattest part of

Pop's roof. Even in the darkness, I can see beds of carrots popping from the soil, and a pond glimmering with moonlight, and *the stars*, Rosie! All those blinking mice above us. My tail shivers in wonderment.

There's a Latin phrase for this, Rosie.

Ad astra per aspera. Through hardship to the stars.

"Oof." Pop drops the basket onto the shingles. He untucks a patchwork quilt from beneath his arm, then spreads it carefully. "Bon appétit."

Of course, Hamlet is already on the scene. Diving. Diving and chomping. Right now, he's attempting to shove a whole spear of asparagus into his mouth—which is a mathematical impossibility. *That is a mathematical impossibility*, I tell him.

Gus peers at Hamlet, his glasses sliding to the tip of his nose. "I'm so happy right now . . . and really sad, too. I can only imagine what you're feeling, Clementine. And Hamlet."

Everything, I tell him with a long blink. *I'm feeling everything*.

Asparagus, Hamlet says. *Chewing asparagus.* He nibbles as millions and millions of stars arc above us. If I ever share these letters with you in order, Rosie, you'll remember: my first step into the outdoors. How the sky reached down and touched the space under my ribs. It told me, *More! More!* There was something *more* that I'd been missing.

It was this.

Rosie?

Is this the last time I'll glimpse the night sky?

Pop breathes out a long sigh, shimmying his nostril hair. Then he gazes at both Gus and me, something unnameable in his eyes. "Gus, remember when I left the table at dinner a few weeks ago? When we went out to that Italian restaurant with your parents?"

"Yeah?" Gus says.

"Your dad was scolding you. About scratching your bike?"

Gus cringes.

"Well," Pop says, "I've been thinking about it ever since. I heard him say that you have 'a mind of your own.' As if it was a terrible thing. The worst thing. And it took every fiber in me not to roar. You perhaps should not have left your eyeglasses on the lounge chair—"

"Definitely not."

"But you can't take one or two small mistakes and say 'this is the sum of a person.' No one else should define you that way. A mind of your own is just that—it's *yours*."

His voice pierces the night air. "All yours. No one else's." He places a hand over Gus's chest, and a finger over mine—right where our hearts are beating. "This, too."

Even Hamlet's listening now. He's stopped chewing the asparagus, cheeks chock-full.

"None of you," he tells us, "have to fit inside someone else's box. You can blaze your own trails. It takes bravery. You have that. It takes creativity. You have that . . . Now, I believe this is about the moment when I give you a pep talk."

This time, I realize he's speaking directly to me.

My neck cranes up, up. His white hair contrasts with the dark sky.

"You and I," Pop says, "are not that different. Well, besides the glaringly obvious. But for a long time—especially when I moved to this country from Greece, when I was seven, even younger than Gus—chess was my language. It's how I got everything up here"—he swirls a hand around his head—"out *there*. Chess makes the inside visible."

Yes.

Yes. That was it.

The inside visible.

"Would you like to know why I quit?" Pop finishes.

Gus holds his breath. I hold my breath.

"Because I was *winning*." Pop laughs a sad laugh. "Winning everything. And it was consuming me. It felt like my only purpose in the world was to play chess. Like if I wasn't playing, if I wasn't winning, I'd die. It's one thing to love the game. It's another to have people believe that you *are* the game. I had newspapers speculating about what I'd do after chess. What would I *be* without chess? Nothing! *Nothing*, they said. Eventually, I started to believe it myself."

He swallows. "But I was a whole person, Clementine. A living, breathing being—not a calculator. Not a machine. I think you can relate to this, yes?"

My throat bobs. *Yes.*

"So, I packed up my boards and my books. I didn't touch them. I vowed that I wouldn't—because my purpose was greater than that. And smaller than that. I wanted to be a better father. I wanted to be a gardener. I wanted to be more than the one thing I was 'good' at. *Good* is such a tricky word. We're often not the ones who decide it. It's a label. It can be a cage. You need to define what it means for yourself."

Good, my mind repeats. A "good" lab mouse. That's all I ever wanted to be. But I never stopped to think about who was defining the word—and if they were right.

Pop's eyes soften, connecting even more deeply with

mine. "But you. But you, little mouse. You've brought the joy back for me. The first time I saw you play, I was afraid, but I started to remember again—why I loved it. Why my brain works the way that it does. I could return to chess without being consumed. So thank you. Sincerely. Thank you."

He picks up one of my tiny paws in his hand, bends down, and presses his forehead to it.

My chest tightens with emotion.

How can I leave him tomorrow, Rosie? How can I leave Gus? Gus, who's breathing next to me. Whose heart is beating. Who's crying now, a tear falling down his cheek. "You have to be okay, Clementine. She's going to be okay, right? This'll work, right? The lab people won't take her away? I'm sorry. I'm sorry. I shouldn't be talking about this!"

Instinctively, I nudge closer to Gus.

Hamlet nudges closer to me.

Pop reaches out and takes Gus's hand. "In my home country, when someone dies, we visit the grave every day for three days. Because on the third day, the soul leaves the body. And for the next forty days and forty nights, we're in a period of mourning. No social events. Rarely leaving the house. My yaya? When my grandfather passed, she wore black until her death—almost thirty years later. Never be afraid to talk about these things, my Gus . . . Now, I think she'll be safe. I think we've done enough. But my point is, no matter what, we'll remember her." His gaze drops again to me. "We'll remember you, Clementine. We'll remember you both. Helping you protect yourself has been one of the greatest honors of my life."

"Me, too," Gus whispers, more tears falling. "Me, too."

Always,

Clementine

Letter 32

Dear Rosie,

I bathed that night, inside a teacup, Gus scrubbing me lightly with a toothbrush. He kept checking the temperature of the water, making sure it was warm enough. (I hate water! The wetness of it! Droplets are great when they're coming from a water bottle, but they're awful behind the ears.) Still, after the scrub, I felt refreshed! Clean! Ready.

Of course, after that, I didn't sleep.

Not a wink!

Gus couldn't sleep, either. Hamlet and I listened, inside the terrarium, as he hugged his binoculars and sighed once. Twice. Eleven times. His sheets rustled with stress, and I thought about curling up, once more, on his shoulder. Letting some of his stress fall on me. I didn't want him to have it. I didn't want Hamlet to have it, either. In the corner, he'd nervously gathered the pieces of his moss scarf, draping it—once more—over his shoulders.

You? he asked around two in the morning, wondering how I was.

Nervous, my tail told him.

Yes, he replied.

What would happen to him, after tomorrow? What would the lab do to him once they knew where we were?

He held up one of his front paws.

Wait, he said, flying behind the miniature Notre Dame Cathedral. Yes, it was still there! Still standing! Moonlight filtered through the tower, brightening the church bell. *Pffft. Pffft.* Hamlet was digging in the catacombs. He dug until he found something. Silence coated the terrarium as, slowly, he emerged—a piece of thread in his hands. *No . . . not a thread?*

A whisker!

Hamlet's broken whisker.

Yours, he told me, offering it with his paws.

I think he'd been keeping it for me. Until I needed it. Until I needed the extra bit of bravery, and wisdom, that a whisker provides. A whisker says *I support you*. A whisker says *Here is a part of me that I'm willingly giving to you*.

I couldn't take it. I just couldn't. Because I wanted the whole of him, always by my side. Couldn't we be together? Couldn't tomorrow save us all?

Yours, he said, gently lifting my elbow, tucking the whisker into my armpit.

He looked so pleased with his gift.

He looked so proud of me.

Ours, I finally said, snuggling up next to him. *Ours*.

Always,

Clementine

Letter 33

Dear Rosie,

The doorbell! My spine jerked at the sound of the doorbell. No, I wasn't asleep. But I was *drifting*, somewhere in that nether space, where my brain likes to whir. Suddenly, I heard footsteps streaming through Pop's front door, humans flooding the house. Hamlet nudged me, the whisker still tucked under my arm, and together we stood on our hind legs, prepared.

"Chess club's here," said Gus, already dressed in one of Pop's button-down shirts. It was six or seven sizes too large and rolled up at the sleeves. He could fit so many mice beneath the fabric. "Man, I didn't know my heart could beat this fast. You just . . . you need to be okay. I know I've messed up a lot of things, but I am *not* going to mess up this. We can do this together."

Together, I said.

"Let's get a move on!" Ginger called up the stairs. When we crested the landing, she tapped the banister with her cane. "We need some time to get a few final rounds of practice in after we set up! I have all my lucky chessboards in the trunk. Don't ask how they're lucky. That's too long of a story. Oh, Marty, stop hyperventilating. You'll be right as a rainstorm."

Marty wheezed as Mei steadied him. "It's just quite a lot of pressure!" he said. "I've never been on TV before, and certainly not for anything this important!"

"It'll run smoothly," Pop assured us, his suit beige and freshly pressed. A tiny bouquet of wildflowers bloomed from his pocket; they looked so small compared to his size. "So smoothly! My crew's setting up in the garden as we speak. Agnes is meeting us there. Not to worry, not to worry."

Except he sounded worried.

"You want a little tinfoil hat?" Gus asked, drifting downstairs to the kitchen. "Don't you like that? Would it make you feel any braver?"

I already had my whisker! Did I need a hat, too?

Gus gave me a wonky-toothed grin, his fear just below the surface. "You're Wondermouse, remember? That's what the news has been calling you. You need a cape or *something*. Here. Would it make you feel better if I wore a hat with you?"

Well, it might. My paws threaded together, deciding. *Okay, yes!*

When Gus started unrolling the tinfoil, Hamlet said, *Huh. Want one.* Mei said she was in if Hamlet was in. Ginger smoothed her feathered jacket and said, "Oh, why the heck not!" In the end, everyone wrapped a sheet of tinfoil around their heads.

A silver lining, for all of us.

"We look absolutely *bonkers*," said Ginger, cackling. "Then again, all the best ones are."

So, Rosie.

So, I said goodbye to Pop's house.

Goodbye, plush rugs and leafy plants. Goodbye, Cheerios boxes and the cabinets and the fridge. Goodbye—

"You'll be back," Gus whispered, stepping outdoors. His throat croaked. "You *will*."

A nervous flutter overtook my stomach.

Was it the last time I'd see these rows of lettuce, these tomato vines? Grass bent under our feet. Willow trees swished. Elbows punching the air with determination, like the first time we met, Gus led us toward the edge of the garden, toward an apple orchard and a pond.

"Beautiful day," said Ginger, sniffing the air. "These

tables are for us, I'm guessing? Marty, you can set down the boards. Wow, look at all these cameras! I feel like a movie star. Make sure they get my best angle. No, not that side! The left side!"

Soon, more commotion.

More scurrying.

New people started arriving, fluttering everywhere on set. Pop greeted each crew member with a clap on the back, explaining that today would be special. Different! "Just follow my lead." Big box lights flickered on—even though the day was already sunny. Cameras swiveled on frames. On the south side of the garden, Mei was combing Hamlet with a very tiny comb, while Gus set me down on the long table.

Chess set after chess set unfurled before me.

It looked like the road to somewhere good.

Remember everything you've learned, I told myself. *Remember the King's Gambit and the Sicilian Defense, the Italian Game and the English Opening. Remember*—

Something's happened.

Something's happening!

Is that another member of the crew? Why's he wearing an all-white suit? With a white hat? With an ice cream cone on it? I'm still on the table, thinking you this letter, but the white-suited man is tiptoeing out from the apple trees. He looks familiar. So familiar. Have we met before?

Realization jolts my tail.

A researcher! A researcher is headed straight for me.

Always,

Clementine

Letter 34

Dear Rosie,

The tinfoil hat didn't help. Hamlet's whisker didn't help. As soon as I glimpsed the researcher—his curled grimace, the grease of his fingertips—my mind traveled back to the lab. I traveled back to who I was: a mouse with almost no control. A lab mouse, who could be picked up by the tail. A lab mouse, who had no choice in her own experiment.

That is all to say, Rosie, I froze.

My tail straightened. My whiskers stiffened.

With deep breaths, Gus was setting up his chess pieces, Pop's vest hanging off his shoulders. He didn't notice at first. But soon, his pupils enlarged to spheres. "No! You can't—"

"*Got* you!" the researcher snapped, grabbing me with both hands.

That's where we are now. Running away from the set! Sprinting through willow trees. His palm is covering my head, my nose—*No! No!* Breathing. I need to breathe. Fighting through fingers—the air, the air. We leap past vegetable boxes, curve around flower beds. Is this happening? Rosie, is this a dream?

Gus is shouting, chasing us as fast as he can. "Clementine! Clementine!" His arms pump. His elbows punch the air. But it isn't enough. It isn't enough. Even when Pop joins in, matching Gus step for step. He's yelling, too.

And it feels so much like when I left you behind! So much like the same thing, all over again. Why don't I ever get to say a real goodbye? Or is this always how a goodbye feels when you're a mouse?

Wiggling, wiggling!

Trembling, trembling.

What do I do? What *can* I do?

Finally, I'm able to poke my head between the researcher's knuckles, my nose sniffing in gusts of air. I look up—and remember him. Everything about him. Crooked eyebrows. The way he sucked his teeth when setting up a microscope. How he picked Hamlet up by the tail, too.

"Stop!" people are yelling in the background.

It's a mix of voices.

Voices, growing softer.

Softer.

Until I can barely hear them at all.

Always,
Clementine

Letter 35

Dear Rosie,

One hundred seconds away from Pop's house, I'm shoved into the ice cream truck. The ice cream truck, Rosie! It smelled of spoiled milk, stickiness, and . . . something else? *Are those my wanted posters?* Dog-eared papers littered the passenger seat. On each one, my face twitched up at the camera, bold letters jumping by my feet. HAVE! YOU SEEN! THIS MOUSE!

"Finally," the researcher breathed. Breathed *on* me, I have to say. At this point, I'd almost given up wiggling, because every time my back legs kicked, the squeeze of his fingers tightened. My rib cage! My stomach! I'm a small mouse for such big hands.

"You can stop struggling now," he told me. "I've caught you, you see? And we're far enough away now. No one's coming for you. No one. It's all over now."

All over?

My fur trembled. Hamlet's whisker quaked between

my paws. It was true: the voices in the background had grown so hushed, I couldn't hear them any longer. Not with my tiny ears. Remember I told you about the sunflowers, Rosie? Remember I told you about my dream? For the last four days, I'd been able to sense those flowers, growing in the space under my ribs. I'd felt *alive*. And now? A hollow sensation creeped in. I was dizzy! Terrified! Confused.

"In you go," the researcher said, trying to shove me into a tiny metal cage.

But my legs splayed out! My paws gripped the sides! My toes curled against the metal.

The researcher grunted, "I told you to *stop*," then gave me a final shove. I stumbled into the darkness—into the metal box. Were cages always this small? *Are they, Rosie?* Could you even stand inside yours? There was barely enough room to raise onto my hind legs.

The door slammed.

The lock clicked.

All this took five seconds.

We were completely gone in six. Tires squeaked like giant mice as the truck rocketed away. I tried to hold on to the bars of the cage, but the acceleration! Too fast! My back slammed against the metal, jolting me, and *No, no! No!* We couldn't be leaving! We couldn't! Had I gotten this all wrong? Am I not playing chess on television? Is this where it ends?

Is this where *I* end?

I clutched Hamlet's whisker, tighter than ever, to my chest—and listened to my heart beat beneath it. *Boom-boom-boom*. Didn't I sound like thunder? Like the first night in Pop's mailbox? Through the booms, something was occurring to me: Hamlet's whisker might be the only thing I had left in the entire world.

Mournfully, I peered down at the tip.

It really was a good whisker. Wiry. Strong. Hamlet-y.

"Wondermouse!" the researcher said, laughing to himself as the truck lurched forward. He was in the driver's seat, more than five feet away from me. But he felt incredibly close. Too close. "Every day on the news, it's Wondermouse this, Wondermouse that. Who came up with that terrible name? Your *identification* is Subject Seven, in case you've forgotten."

My ears shook and my whiskers trembled. *Clementine!*

Isn't my name *Clementine*?

"I'm going to be a hero back at the lab," he continued, fingers dancing across the steering wheel. His whole body bounced. "I almost didn't think we'd catch you! Man! We checked everywhere—the woods, the fields, all the businesses on main street. Every house this side of town. We even brought in those search-and-rescue dogs to track your scent, and the lab rented this surveillance truck. Nice disguise, isn't it? It's got ice cream in the back, to really *sweeten* the deal. Ha, ha. Get it? *Get it?*" Through the metal bars, I could see him grin. "Even with the truck, we hit a dead end. Or we thought we did. And *then*, out of nowhere, one of our motion-activated cameras catches something. We set up cameras everywhere, you know. There were two in Whisper Creek Park."

The words hit me like water.

Like being dropped into a cold tub.

The researcher let out a chuckle. "You putting it together? I can't see your smart little face, but I'm guessing you are. That chess club of yours? We saw you wiggling in a pocket, on film, and then, when the kid took off, a bunch of others followed. We tracked a license plate for a Miss Ginger Sutherbee . . . all the way . . . to that house." He said the final words slowly, tauntingly, trying to catch a glimpse of me while driving. With one hand, he grabbed an ice cream bar from the dashboard and leisurely unwrapped it. Globs of vanilla trailed down his hand, chocolate wafers squishing as he bit them. "I should've never left that first time. I knew something was fishy! Mousy, more like it."

So that was it.

This is it? This is it, Rosie? A quiver travels up my tail, and I feel very cold. Very, very cold. Even my toes shiver. Is this the last letter I'll ever write? What happens now? Will I get one final meal? A brussels sprout? Even a tiny one? Will I see you one last time, before it's all over—so that I can tell you everything? Tell you all these letters, organized inside my head?

Or . . . will you never . . . get the chance to hear them? Will they . . . stay trapped . . . in my brain? My brain, under a microscope?

I slump back inside the cage. I'm slumping back, Rosie. My ears are flat against my head.

Gus told me that it never ends well for mice in stories.

I guess . . . I just thought . . . that I could be different.

Always,

Clementine

Letter 36

Dear Rosie,

A lab mouse is obedient. A lab mouse has a purpose. A lab mouse is for science. But a lab mouse has a nose for sniffing and ears for hearing and eyes for seeing. A lab mouse has paws for playing chess and whiskers for catching dew and a tail for balancing on succulents. A lab mouse has a heart beating beneath her ribs.

This is what I'm thinking.

This is what I'm telling you.

I don't know.

I'm not sure it matters now.

I've never felt so small to myself.

Always,

Clementine

Letter 37

Dear Rosie,

If this is my last letter, I should tell you everything—even if you'll never hear it. Doesn't a letter count, even if it never makes it to the reader? I'll feel better knowing that these memories are there, somewhere.

So here it is.

Brussels sprouts are best fresh; humans cook them, sometimes, but the crisp should be there. Sunflower seeds are a close second when it comes to crunch. Mathematically, time travel requires a minimum speed of 187,282 miles per second. Starry nights reach inside you. A vegetable garden has the greatest colors. Anyone can play chess, even a mouse. Even a chimpanzee. Anyone can write a letter, because letters are just our thoughts, organized, for someone else to read.

Chimpanzees make excellent friends.

Humans can be good.

Mice are always smarter than you expect.

"Don't even *think* about trying to get out of that cage," the researcher says as he turns up the radio. He's singing off-key, offbeat. "*Wooo-hooo! Waaaa-haaaa! Ooooh, yeah. I know you were escaping in the lab at night. We saw it when we played back the security footage. Waaaa-haaaa!* But this lock's impenetrable. No prizing it free!"

The scent of him is wafting into the passenger's seat. Chemicals. Sulfur. Grease. It mixes with the scents from the back: bitter chocolate ice cream, frozen vanilla, synthetic strawberry. Coughing a little, the researcher lowers the windows a crack.

"And no Felix to help you! Bet you think I didn't know about that, either? I haven't been able to pin him down *for sure*, but you can never trust a Canadian . . . He's been feeding fruit to that chimpanzee."

Is it possible for ears to droop and perk at the same time?

Mine do.

Rosie?

In all my letters, I never imagined what you'd say back. What would your letters look like if you wrote some? Would you sign them with your fingers? Would you write in pencil, gray swirls against the page? Maybe you'd *hoot* them. Maybe you'd dance them.

What would you say to me now?

The car is speeding down a dirt road. Dust puffs every-where, enormous clouds of it. Clouds! From the tightness of my cage, my paws pressed to the bars, I stare up, out the window, and breathe big into my little chest. Morning light strokes the edges of my face.

What would you look like, Rosie, in the sun?

You'd look . . . you'd look like an Outside Chimpanzee.

Like you were always an Outside Chimpanzee—who just got stuck.

Who got trapped.

Your fingers? They're for dipping into pools of honey, for scooping up sweet figs. Your arms are for swinging in branches. Your feet should be splashing in shallow water on a hot day. None of you was made for a cage.

Here is another thing about letters, Rosie. If you write, you exist. If you're writing your own story, then you're telling your own story. You're not letting anyone else say it for you.

Other people have been telling our stories for so long.

We're like pawns in a game.

And we have always deserved more.

Stay with me, I'd tell you if you were here, *just for another second.*

Your tired eyes would look out the window, then back to my face. *Always*, you'd tell me. *Always, Clementine.*

Part III

Endgame

Letter 38

Dear Rosie,

Except . . . it doesn't end there. Because there's a breeze.

The passenger-side window right above me! It's *open*. Neck craning up, I notice a mouse-size sliver just at the top. Wind pulses by.

"A few more minutes," the researcher says giddily to himself. He bounces in his seat. "We're so close. Do you think they'll promote me to lab manager? Capturing Wondermouse must have some perks besides the reward money. First thing I'll do, I'll fire Felix, and . . . Darn it, red light. When are they going to fix the traffic lights in this town?"

As the ice cream truck slows to a halt, my head tilts even more as I examine the window. Examine the Outside. I picture my front toes knocking against the glass, a tap that sounds like *go, go*. But how *can* I go, considering that I'm stuck here in this cage? I start shivering again. My mind tries to wander toward safer topics:

the Pythagorean theorem and brussels sprouts and the fourth move in the Queen's Gambit. Anything to distract me from my fate at the lab.

"Come on, come *on*," the researcher growls at the traffic light.

I still have time in my life. Just a little bit of time left. And I want to think of you, Rosie. Whiskers tilting toward the sunlight, I close my eyes and let myself remember it once more: the first moment I slipped between the bars of your cage, all those nights ago, in the lab. There were no wood shavings. Only metal, like my cage right now. You'd given me a funny look, amber eyes flickering. I hadn't been able to read it then. Not fully. We were still learning to understand each other.

But . . . now?

Now! I can read it now. Finally, finally, I understand.

If you can slip between *the bars,* your eyes said, *why don't we slip out?*

Time slows in the ice cream truck as realization hits me. My front paws fly to the space above my heart, and I stagger back, eyes bulging. You're right, Rosie! You're right! All this time, I've wanted to stay alive. Alive, I might see you again. Yet I never imagined *how* we'd meet. What if . . . what if we could reunite and be *out*? Away from our cages?

Both of us, free.

Peering up at the cracked-open window, I blink furiously. My brain pounds. Thoughts arrive like sparks of light. I learned chess, didn't I? I learned to survive on the Outside, taking steps that I wanted. The researchers taught me that my intelligence is for humans. That my life is for science. But maybe . . . maybe my life is *mine*?

"Green, green, *green*," the researcher urges the stoplight. "One more second and I'm just going to run it! We're getting you to the lab no matter what."

No, a voice squeaks inside me.

It's my own.

My own voice, Rosie! My own life.

"This is ridiculous," the researcher says, shifting in his seat. Vinyl whines beneath him. His hands have a death grip on the steering wheel, and the music seems to louden. *Boom! Boom! Boom!* "Okay, I'm going."

Standing up on my hind legs inside the cage, I decide: I'm going, too! Because we're more than just pawns, Rosie.

We can move our own pieces.

The car inches forward, and so do I—toward the door of the cage. This has become a chess game. A giant chess game! And I already know my opening.

Reaching out, I test one of the bars, shaking it a little

with my paw. This cage isn't steel. It's flimsy. The lock looks flimsy, too.

Okay, pick! I need a pick for the lock.

Thinking, I scratch my chin with Hamlet's whisker, and . . . Oh! Of course! Hamlet, thank you! The end of the whisker is pointy. Perfectly pointy. Eagerly, I slip it into the lock, hoping to get the angle just right. Jiggling. Jiggling. Twisting—

The lock falls open with a sharp *snap!*

"What was that sound?" the researcher says, checking the cage—still five feet away from me. Panic quivers his voice, and another glob of ice cream drips down his hand. "Why do I smell raspberries? Subject Seven? Subject Seven, what are you doing? Don't you even think about . . . *No!*"

Yes!

Paws first, I push the cage door open and spring free, landing on the long seat—just out of the researcher's reach. Then I'm climbing, climbing high to the top of the seat, the vinyl slick under my toes.

"You! Will! Not!"

The researcher's hand swipes in my direction; he's trying to inch across the roadway, save his ice cream sandwich, and catch me simultaneously—but I'm too quick! Too motivated! I'm thinking ahead and reading my opponent and remembering everything—everything that Gus and Pop taught me. Everything that Hamlet taught me. I'm remembering everything that was already *in* me, that's been with me since I was born.

The headrest? I'll use the passenger-side headrest! That'll work if I get this angle right, too. Frantically, I make the three-inch leap from vinyl to glass, toes gripping the window's edge. I'm dangling! My tail's windmilling! The researcher's grasping at me, leaning across the seat to clip my back legs with his fingers, so it's time. Time to jump. I teeter there on the glass ledge, glancing at the long way down. The black road stretches out beneath me. And then—

We're moving.

The truck is moving again!

"You've *lost*!" the researcher says, stomping the gas. The truck speeds faster, faster. "It's over, Subject Seven! You're supposed to be smart but—"

Goodbye!

I jump for both of us, Rosie, my tail spinning through the summer air. Warmth greets my fur as I spread my arms wide, floating. Practically hanging in the sky! It feels so free! It feels—

Splat!

I've miscalculated a little, and hit a telephone pole, midjump.

Very lightly.

My paws flatten against it, belly sliding down the surface. With the *splat*, I think I might've discovered half a mathematical formula for time travel. I also think that I need to run. Shaking my ears to clear my head, I watch the ice cream truck—now a block ahead of me—swerve to a halt. Exhaust mushrooms behind it.

And I rush forward, away from the truck, speeding in a line at the edge of the road. Cars are flitting by me. Blue cars! Yellow cars! Running, running, I try to glance under them, try to figure out exactly where I am.

Look! Buildings!

Oh!

I've seen them before, from inside the wicker basket of Gus's bike. If I hurry along this road, skidding right then left, I'll be down the street from Whisper Creek Park. But it's a long way for a mouse to travel on foot. On paw. Can I really make it back to Pop's house in half an hour? Will they start the show without me? Will they—?

"SUBJECT SEVEN!"

The researcher's voice lifts over the road noise. Briefly, my neck cranes while running, and I clock that he's turned off his engine. His head (and the rest of him!) is leaning out the window. "How on earth did you get out of that? You better stay right there so I—"

I should run faster, okay, okay, *zoom!* Cutting across two lanes of traffic—a very advanced-level maze—I pitter-patter onto the main street. Now, paws against the sidewalk. Darting around people with bags. Whizzing past window displays. Summer sun beats down. Left. Turning left.

(I'm going to concentrate for two or three seconds.)

(I hope that's okay.)

(It's difficult to write a letter and escape.)

Always,

Clementine

Letter 39

Dear Rosie,

Now, where was I?

This is what happens next.

So fast, my eyes scan the area, reading a few signs. BUS STOP. FLOWER SHOP. Then, the word SUPERMARKET flashes bright green in the morning air. Underneath it, glass doors swoosh open and closed, open and—*I'm going! I'm going inside.* That's what I decide. Isn't this in the right direction? Can't I cut through the store? Isn't the—

"Stop! Subject Seven, stop or I'll—"

Of course, I don't stay to hear the rest of it! Zipping, zooming, I navigate around splotches of gum, around half-broken toothpicks on the ground, right up to the swishy, whooshing doors. Scientifically, these should open! Why aren't they opening? Am I too small to trigger the sensor? *Hurry! Hurry!* Several hundred feet behind me, the researcher is running in my direction, hands already open to catch me, but—

A cart!

A shopping cart glides by me, so I spring and swing, settling just above the wheel. Noises whir loudly in my ears: the sound of the cart, the sound of the store, the buzzing and the humming and the dinging. And so many colors! My brain doesn't know what to settle on first. Row after row of oranges! Sparkling apples in red-and-pink towers! Tin cans stacked like pyramids.

"STOP THAT MOUSE!"

Right. I'm afraid I got distracted there for a second, Rosie. Even when you're being chased, fruit can throw you off track! Ears back, my front paws reach for the ground, and I dive off the cart by a mound of two-for-one potatoes. They smell earthy and good, and I back into them, tail first, for just a moment. I need to think very quickly. I need to *move* very quickly. There must be an exit at the back of the store! That way! That's the way back to Pop's place, to the broadcast! If I scurry faster than I've ever scurried, can I make it in time?

Go!

Out from the potatoes! Onto the clean, white tile. A sea of legs greets me. Human after human after human, all picking through the vegetable aisle. I'm a small mouse. Smaller than average, even. So I need to be higher, less stomp-able. I climb! My tiny claws dig into a pack of cardboard boxes and—*Oh, are those raisins? Are those toma-toes?* Never mind! Using my tail for balance, I tiptoe along the edge of the cherry tomato stand. Does this tinfoil hat provide enough coverage? Can anybody see me?

An answer arrives soon enough!

"Mouse," a man says calmly, selecting a small yellow onion. Then he takes another look at me, our eyes locking, and screeches. "*Mouse!* Mouse in the tomaaaaaaaaaatoes!"

"Where?" another man says, head whipping around.

He, too, spots me.

And that's when everything descends into chaos. Now three people are screaming—little pops of: *Ah! Bah! Ah!* Everyone in the vegetable aisle begins checking under their feet, as if I'll materialize beneath them, and the researcher skids across the tile, heading straight for the tomatoes! I'm on an island! Isolated, trapped again, except for . . .

BRUSSELS SPROUTS!

Oh, Rosie!

Rosie! I can't tell you how joyful I am to see them. Not because I'm hungry (although I *always* have room for a brussels sprout, as they're so chewy in the middle, and delicious), but because they're *tall*. They grow on a *stalk*, sprout-y bulbs sticking out like rungs in a ladder. With half a second to spare, mind spinning, I think: *Tail!*

The researcher lunges forward, sweating, hands outspread.

His fingertips graze my back as I speed over the tomato hill, into the onion valley, and finally straight up the sprout ladder. Above me, a thin piece of metal mists water on the vegetables, keeping them slippery and fresh—and it is *perfect*! Perfect for an escape.

"Don't!" the researcher says.

But I'm already leaping. Leaping with such profound momentum. Leaping like a mouse acrobat! Midair, I spin so my tail can catch me. It wraps around the vegetable mister—which feels nice actually. So cool and so refreshing. Yet, that's not the point. What was my point? Oh, yes . . . I swing.

Upside down, I can see the researcher knocking into grocery store shoppers, who are so entranced by the swinging mouse they hardly budge. "Out of my way!" he's crying. "She is a *very* important lab specimen!"

A voice on the intercom tells everyone, "Valued shoppers! Please stay calm! We assure you that there's no need to . . . Wow! She's really going for it! We're watching on the security camera, and I've . . . never seen a mouse do that before . . . STAY CALM, SIR!"

On his hands and knees, the researcher is scrambling over the tomatoes, squashing them, reaching out, and—

I let go!

I'm flying! Flying, away! Or rather, flying across the aisle, into the cereal section. My body smacks into a box of Cheerios (*Oh, Cheerios, my old friend!*), but I quickly recover—and speed away. Now, it is a race. Now, the real rush begins.

"Don't let her get away!" the researcher screams.

The sound of his voice travels all the way up my tail, and suddenly my whiskers curl back. My paws pitter-patter faster, faster—across the bran flakes and the healthy oats and the crispy clusters. *Back! Back!* Back to Pop's. *Rosie, Rosie, Rosie.* I say your name with each step, with every heartbeat, two hundred times a second. I've come so far! And I have a chess game to play!

But the researcher is gaining on me no matter how quickly I skitter. For every step he jumps, I have to run twenty. Or thirty? Or forty? And then he starts swiping! Swatting the cereal boxes! Knocking them from shelves, trying to catch me!

"SIR!" the intercom says. "Bran flakes are buy-one-get-one, but you don't have to be so EAGER!"

It appears as if everything—absolutely everything—is gaining sound. Even the tops of jam jars seem loud as I hopscotch across them, tail flailing. The lids make a *plink, plink.* The *bum-bum-bum* of background music becomes a *thrum-thrum-thrum*. Shoes squeal against the tile, super-market workers rushing toward me with mops. Mops? To clean me? I'm already clean?

"CLEMENTINE!"

Mid-run, my head whips around.

Gus!

It's *Gus*!

Pop soon follows—then Mei, then Marty . . . and then Ginger! Ginger, on a motorized scooter with a shopping cart attached. Her cane flails wildly as she lets out a "Yee-haw!" All five of them wear their tinfoil hats, the metal sparkling under the supermarket lights.

And Hamlet?

Is that Hamlet?

Perched on the rim of Ginger's cart, his whole body angles forward like he's leading the charge.

For the first time in my life, I'm speechless.

These people, this mouse . . .

They think I'm worth something. Something more.

"CLEMENTINE, KEEP GOING!" Gus bellows, charg-ing further into the store. Because, oh! Right! Running! I've paused for half a second too long, just enough time for the researcher to snatch the tip of my tail. Instantly, I remember the feeling. The yanking. The lifting me up by my most sensitive part.

So I bite him.

This time, I bite him.

Which is not what a lab mouse does.

But I am not a lab mouse anymore.

"You *little*—" the researcher says, yanking his hand back, shaking it. And I think: *Yes! Little! Little but mighty.* Then I dive into a gap between jam jars, wiggling until I reach the bottom of the shelf. Hidden! Invisible! Through the packaging, the smell of . . . strawberry? Grapes? And . . . ha! Raspberry jelly.

"SPLIT UP!" I hear Ginger say. "Divide and conquer! Together, we'll make it out alive!"

"Well," Pop adds, "we'll definitely make it out *alive.* Marty! You and I go down the toilet paper aisle! Gus and . . ." The rest of his words blend into the sound of sirens. There are sirens now! An alarm, blaring in the background. *BLEEP! BLEEP!*

"Security!" the loudspeaker announces. "Security is on the way to aisle two! Do not run! Stop running! I SAID STOP RUNNING, EVERYONE! And ma'am? MA'AM! You cannot use that apple as a weapon!"

Aisle two? Is that my aisle? Where is Gus? Where is Mei? Is Ginger still flailing her cane? Where does this hole lead? Squeezing my body into the circle, I crawl between aisles, shimmying into a stack of toilet paper. Weaving,

weaving, weaving between the rolls. My paws pick over bags of cotton balls, over the bristles of kitchen brushes, until I reach the end. The end of the shelving! Should I hide here, I wonder, waiting for Gus to find me? Or should I rush toward that cracked-open door? Another sign, right past the fish counter, flashes EMERGENCY EXIT.

This is an emergency, isn't it?

Noises grow—more *bleep*s, more shouts—when I peek my whiskers into the air. No researcher here? Not in this aisle?

"THERE!" someone shouts.

Me?

"YOU!" the researcher yells. Twisting my gaze, I see him bolt into the paper aisle, but Ginger is right at his heels. Her motorized cart lets out a violent *whir* as she lurches forward, Hamlet at the helm, and trips the researcher with her cane. The researcher stumbles, catching himself on a rack of dish soap, and—

Leap!

Toward the emergency exit. Toward Pop's garden. As soon as my toes hit the tile, Gus appears, pushing through the crowd. His tinfoil hat wobbles on his head. "Run, run, run!" he says, trailing close behind me. It almost feels as if I'm in the maze again, leading another mouse. *This way! Follow!*

Is Gus's heart beating as fast as mine?

(No. Physically impossible. But it might be close!)

"My bike's over by that tree!" he breathes, bursting outside, shoes slapping against the concrete. "The other tree! No, the *other* other tree! Everyone else took Ginger's minivan but I thought it would be quicker if I took a shortcut through the woods because I knew you were headed to the lab, and then everyone caught up and saw you jump from that car! You are the bravest mouse I've ever met!"

Simultaneously, we skid to a stop, and Gus squashes a helmet over his tinfoil hat, then lifts me into the basket. "I'm so, so sorry that he got you, though! That guy just came out of *nowhere*, but if we really hurry, we can still make it back before the live show, and . . . There he is!"

The researcher slams through the emergency exit.

Oh!

My tail curls in the basket.

And Gus takes off, pedals whirring, his words lifting over the wind. "I promised to protect you! And I haven't given up on that. I'll never give up on that!" He speeds forward. "Let's see how fast we can go."

So, we are fast—together.

Always,

Clementine

Letter 40

Dear Rosie,

I'm writing to you from the basket. Outside, there are millions upon millions of leaves. Millions of blades of grass. An infinite amount of sky. I wish you were seeing all of it! I wish you could feel the wind through the wicker gaps! Wouldn't it flutter your chin hair? Wouldn't you like that?

"Just . . . another . . . minute," Gus pants, as we cut a hard right into a field. My whole body tilts, unbalanced. Sunflower stalks snap under the bike tires. "We'll . . . get there."

An optimist, I think. Gus is an optimist, too.

Clawing my way up to the basket's edge, I let my nose peek into the sun. Farmland unfolds around us. So many greens! So much orange! Six days ago, I didn't understand that colors could be this colorful, and now? Now, Rosie, I picture what it might look like if we ever meet again. You'll . . . hoot. That's it. You'll hoot when you see me, even though I'm small, nearly hidden in the grass. You'll knuckle-walk in my direction, and we'll eat fruit together. All the fruit we can. *Clementine*, you'll sign with your fingers—because you'll remember my name.

Who knows how many letters I have left?

Who knows how this will end?

But . . . Oh.

Oh.

I do have an idea.

"He's not following us?" Gus asks, neck craning. "Please . . . tell me he's not following us. I took a shortcut, and then another shortcut, but there aren't any more trails here, unless we make one . . . *Whoa!* Is that car following us? Is that another researcher? It *looks* like it could be. Gah! Stay down, Clementine! Stay down!"

Teeth chattering, I dip a little lower in the basket, grabbing on to the edge as we plow left. Twigs smack the sides of Gus's helmet. Thankfully, he has double protection! The tinfoil is useful after all!

"There's a creek behind Pop's garden!" Gus shouts. "Well, there used to be! It dried up . . . but there's still this big gully . . . and I think we're going to have to jump it!"

My tail stiffens again as I see where we're headed. Not too far in the distance, the land dips and disappears. Like someone has scooped out a long cut of earth. And it looks . . . wide. Over ten feet wide! We can't jump that gully. The trajectory, the mathematics—it just doesn't compute!

Gus wheezes out the next words. "If I go all the way around the garden . . . we won't make it in time! And that car will definitely catch us!" *Pedaling! Faster! Faster!* "You . . . remember? How Pop said we're meant to blaze our own trails? I think . . . I think we're literally going to have to do that right now!"

You sure?

"I'm sure! Now . . . HOLD ON, CLEMENTINE!"

Oh! Right.

"AND DON'T LOOK DOWN!"

I look down! Below us, bike tires whizz into a blur as we gather speed. More speed. More! Then, suddenly, we're airborne. A petrified squeak builds in my chest as the gully unfolds. It's a steep drop! A very steep drop! For a tenth of a second, we're hovering over it—over the valley of driftwood and dirt, ferns growing in the shade—and all I can do is wonder: *Has a mouse ever soared this high?* Momentum propels us forward, yet I start to feel a drop in my stomach. Falling! Down! We're going down!

I lean back in the basket, teeth chattering, bracing myself for impact . . .

But we land safely, on the other side of the gully, bike

tires thudding in the summer grass. Rosie! We're alive!

"He'll never be able to pass over that!" Gus bursts out. "Not in a big car like that! We're safe! You're safe now! We did it! Well, we *almost* did it . . . There's still the whole chess thing. And the saving you from the rest of the lab thing. And the . . . Where is everyone? Didn't they make it back?"

Our bike tires screech. We stagger to a stop around the corner of Pop's garden.

Just by the mailbox.

(*Goodbye, mailbox*, if we never see each other again.)

Gus clutches the sides of his face. "What if they got hurt at the supermarket or something? What if we just left them there and—"

"WE'RE HERE!" Ginger bellows, careening around the corner in her minivan. Her voice echoes through the glassy windows as the vehicle bulldozes straight into the mailbox. There's a tremendous *crunch*, then a parade of mail scattering to the dirt.

Pop quickly slides out of the passenger seat, white hair pluming behind him. "Oh my. We'll . . . worry about that later."

Ginger follows, along with Marty, Mei, and Hamlet. "Pshaw!" she says, examining the wreckage. "Who writes letters nowadays anyhow? Come on, don't we have some mice to save? Our audience awaits!"

Awaits! Hamlet says, as if he's just learned a new word and is busy testing it out.

We rush into the driveway, Pop asking if we're all right, if we're hurt, if we really jumped a ravine on a two-speed bicycle. "Are you bleeding anywhere?" he says, patting his pockets as if he's searching for something—and can't quite remember what. "Do you need medical assistance? Or a cup of tea? We'll have to hurry. Hurry, hurry! Apparently Agnes has just arrived on set. We're live in two minutes!" A whole conversation occurs with only his eyebrows, as they elaborately wiggle up and down. "Two minutes! Two minutes! Quick. We've called in extra security, but the researcher might return . . ."

"He'll be a *little* while," Ginger says, winking. "Supermarket security got him right as he was busting through the exit. Said he was inciting a riot! And trying to steal the tomato cans!"

Soon, grass buckles under our feet. We speed-walk by the beehive and the tomatoes and the blueberry bushes. We zip past the apple orchard and the sunflowers and the yellow patch of land waiting for pumpkins to grow.

Now, the cameras.

Now, the chessboards, laid out like a maze.

It's happening.

It's happening!

Near the end of the long table, Ginger is already yelling, "Places! Places, my darlings!"

We're all here. Gus in his too-big vest. Mei in her cat-ear headband. Quickly, Pop attaches microphones to their clothes, smooths the wrinkles from his own suit, and tosses a final look in my direction.

He gives me one last wink, which I catch. And hold close to me.

"Live in five, four, three . . ." a camerawoman says.

I'm doing this for you, Rosie.

Two, she signals.

I hope it's enough.

One, she signals.

"Hello," Pop says, beard glimmering in the August sun. "Welcome to my garden."

Always,

Clementine

Letter 41

Dear Rosie,

How are you? Are you listening? Have they pulled out a television, somewhere in the middle of the lab? Maybe someone's flipping through the channels. Maybe they pause on *Pop's Hobbies*, and they spot something gray in the background. No, not something—some*one*. A tiny mouse, tiptoeing past a solitary rook, making her way to the edge of the board.

Do you see me?

Do you see us?

As Pop explains where Gus found me (in the mailbox), I inch toward Hamlet. Just in case you're watching, Rosie, I wave—and Hamlet flexes his tail, too, arcing a *Hello*. Of course, he's not facing the cameras, so he ends up waving to a mulberry bush at the center of the garden. But I spin him around, telling him *thank you*. For the whisker. For the escape. In response, he touches the space where the whisker once sprouted just below the fur, and suddenly there's a pleased spark in his eyes.

He's a good lab mouse, Rosie.

No, a good *mouse*.

The lab was never us.

"As you can see," Pop is saying, "today's program is going to be very special. I'm not sure there's been anything like it in history. Normally I'd say 'Welcome, friends.' But today, I'm going to change it up a bit!" He shimmies his eyebrows. "Hello, friends and potential enemies . . .'"

"Psst," Gus whispers to me, bouncing on his toes. Should I try that? Should I bounce? Does it help the nerves? "I just wanted to say, in case I don't get a chance to say it later: You can *do* this, Clementine. You might be the smartest mouse ever, but you're a lot more than that, too. You're a trailblazer."

"Go get 'em," whispers Ginger, leaning in.

Then there's Mei, mouthing: *Good luck, Clementine!*

It's starting to feel like a dream. Like this is not quite real. All the cameras and the lights, the microphones, and the music in the background. But Hamlet's here. Hamlet's real. He nudges me, a glassy look on his face.

So, I say.

Huh, he says.

And then it begins.

"Seven-time state chess champion!" Pop bellows to the cameras, hands fluttering. "She once pinned the late, great Boris Nikolayev in just fifteen moves! Everyone, may I introduce to you—my brilliant friend, Agnes Rota."

A round of applause makes me jump.

Just a little jump.

But I wring my tail and wonder if I should sit down? Or keep standing? Agnes approaches me hesitantly, her feet shuffling through the grass. She's small like Gus, with gray hair that frizzles around her in waves. The camera follows her. It follows her footsteps and her swinging arms and her wide eyes as she notices me. "Kristo?" she says to Pop, like a question. "I thought that you and I were . . . What's going on?"

I bow.

Just a little bow.

(I am, after all, a tiny mouse.)

"This," Pop explains, pointing to me with a steady finger, "is your competitor, Clementine. While you were backstage, I explained everything to our audience at home. This marvelous little creature? You may know her better as Wondermouse. So sorry I couldn't tell you beforehand. We wanted to make sure everyone knew this wasn't staged. This is real! This is live!"

"Wondermouse . . ." Agnes says slowly, squinting behind a pair of thick black glasses. "Wondermouse is going to play me at chess?"

Pop taps the tip of his nose. "Precisely. She's going to play *all* of us at chess. To show exactly how brilliant she is."

I hold myself tall, my chin high.

Then, a gentle smile breaks onto Agnes's face. "Well, this is . . . just about the best thing ever. I'm shocked, but I've heard quite a great deal about you, brilliant mouse." Frizzy gray hair blowing in the breeze, she extends a hand in my direction. A handshake? For me? "We always shake before a match."

As my paw fits between two of her fingers, my chin raises even higher. (Hamlet sticks his in, too—for good measure. His paw. Not his chin.)

"Then let's get this show on the road!" Pop thunders. "Thirty minutes for the program, so thirty minutes on the clock! Players, ready? Everyone promise to do their best? To play as if you were playing a human? Wonderful! Begin! *Go!*"

Suddenly, all the pieces seem taller. I'm wavering here, on the first board, and the bishops are growing. The rooks are growing. Everything looks so *large*. So unfit for a mouse.

With trembling fingers, Gus moves his pawn to e4. He

thunks it in the space, as always, and the sound brings me back to this moment. To the solid board beneath my toes. To Hamlet, cheering from the sidelines. I didn't realize it, but he'd kept a bit of the white tissue from Gus's pocket. Had he been storing it in his cheeks? Now he's using it like a flag. *Swoosh! Swoosh!* In the air!

"You can do this, Clementine," Gus repeats. "It's all you."

My heart thunks like the chess piece.

But I bend over. I push one of my pawns, driving forward with my toes.

Quickly! Quicker! Hopping to the next board, over to Ginger—who slides out a knight. Over to Mei, who begins with a pawn. Is Agnes trying to play the Sicilian Defense? Is Pop going with the Italian? Scurrying from board to board, I'm remembering those books on tape. I'm remembering swinging in my hammock, staring at the walls of the terrarium and thinking about Bobby Fischer. And Garry Kasparov. And Mikhail Tal. All the greatest chess players who ever lived.

What did they have on the line?

Who were they playing for?

One by one, each human makes their opening move. The camera tracks me as I counter. Three moves in. Four moves in. Fifteen. And Pop narrates, "Splendid openings from Clementine! Yet, the middle game is where she's historically had trouble. Let's see what she does against Marty, the man in the green cap . . . Oh! *Oh!* Looks like she's bringing out her queen! Is she going to . . . ? She's pinned him! She's pinned him! One player down, five to go. Anyone who thought this would be an easy match for the humans, think again."

Marty! Hamlet says, waving his miniature flag. He smells of raspberries, too.

I stop as Marty stands, then bows to me while tipping his hat. And for a second, I feel those sunflowers, Rosie. The ones I told you about. The ones growing right beneath my ribs, right where my heart is beating. I pause, taking a second. (A second can be a long time if you're a mouse. I am little. So I appreciate little things.) Marty and I hold each other's gaze—his green eyes to my black—and I try to tell him I'm thankful.

Should I bow, too?

Yes!

I arch forward, one paw at my waist.

Then I'm skittering again, flying, the table slippery under my toes. Even though we're outside in a garden, even though there are cameras and noises and voices, I only hear chess. I'm only listening to the *thud*s and the *thunk*s and the *slide*s. It's very loud in my tiny ears.

"She's gone for the King's Gambit," Pop narrates,

"against my grandson, Gus, and she's continued to follow that down the board. Against me, she's attempting a rarer variation. The Scandinavian Defense. I'm not sure if this is something she practiced, or something that's just come to her right now—"

Now, I say, with a flick of my tail, finishing my game with Ginger.

"Oh, *drat*!" she says, clucking her tongue. "I mean, it's good that you're winning and everything, mouse, but good golly, I wish I'd seen that one coming. I would've said something other than 'good golly,' but I'm led to believe this is a wholesome television program for children."

"Two down!" Pop says. "Four to go."

Mei moves next.

Then Gus. Then Pop.

Agnes shuffles a bishop across the board and murmurs to herself, "Something smells like raspberries."

I'm summoning everything from the last six days. Every early-morning practice session with Gus. Every moment at night with Hamlet as variations and gambits glowed in my brain. Is this my purpose? Right now? When Felix dropped me in the mailbox that first night, he said the word *purpose*. How I'm not meant to die.

But I think a purpose is even wider than that.

I think I was born to take deep breaths. And investigate

my life. And meet people. And meet you. I think I was born for something other than what I was bred for. Here's another thought, Rosie: if someone is telling you what you have to be, then you might lose the opportunity to be what you are.

"Ooof," Gus says, laughing. "That was an *attack*! You went for it! Awesome job, Clementine. I'm really proud of you. Really, really proud . . ." A different sort of emotion rolls into his voice now. It sounds like hope. "I resign, my friend."

He tips his king over on the board.

It makes a hollow sound.

And I'm thinking, Rosie, that it's very difficult to write a letter and play several chess games at once. But I'm trying to concentrate, I'm trying to remember everything, I'm trying. Will you hear me? Do you understand? That everything I'm about to do is for you?

"Looks like we're making our way to the endgame," Pop says, "with only myself, Agnes, and Mei left . . . Okay, that's Mei down. She put up an exceptional fight! All right . . . Hmmm, Clementine's just traded herself out of a tricky position. I thought I might've bested her on the diagonal, but . . . Beautiful work. Absolutely beautiful work. I resign, too."

Another king, tipping.

Another sound.

Pop reaches over to shake my paw. His hands are warm and trembly, and far bigger than my own. My paw sits just at the edge of his finger. "I mean this with the utmost sincerity," he says, staring deep into my eyes. "You've surpassed every expectation or hope that I had for you. I've never seen anyone learn chess with such precision in six days—let alone a mouse. You are a genius. But more than that, you are *you*. Bravo. Bravo."

Can whiskers grow with pride? The tips of mine feel tingly, longer somehow, as I scurry to the final board—only five minutes left on the clock.

Have I done enough? Are viewers seeing what I'm seeing? That I'm more than the lab? That you're more than the lab? That we all deserve more?

Abruptly, Agnes takes my knight.

I don't see it coming.

I'm already four pieces down. She's in a stronger position.

Mei bites her thumbnail in the background, and from the corner of my eye, I catch Gus nervously fiddling with a piece of string from Pop's vest pocket. Are they worried about me? Should I be worried? Should I have seen that coming? Or *this*, as she captures my rook? Five pieces down. Four minutes to go.

I take a small sip of water from the tiny bowl by the board.

I splash some on my face, trying to think of a way out of the maze, too. What about the Austrian Gambit? How can I surprise her? How can I push this queen? Back on the board, my legs slip against the marble. My tail is a bit limp as I shuffle between two pawns. And when I try to move my next piece, it's . . . it's heavy. So heavy, suddenly.

I'm so tired.

It's too much for one mouse . . .

Hamlet?

Hamlet's on the board?

He's cresting the edge of it, teetering over to the queen. And his paws are next to my paws. He's pushing alongside me, tissue bits chomped in his mouth. Together, we *swish* the queen along the diagonal. We trade a knight for a rook. We advance farther and farther down the board— until our pawn, our tiny pawn, becomes a bishop again.

Little by little, Agnes begins to lean back in her chair.

She's realizing something.

She's smiling.

With twenty seconds left, she looks both me and Hamlet in the eyes. "Brilliant," she says. "I've never seen a recovery quite like that. I've never seen a *game* quite like that. I resign with gratitude, awe . . . and just a hint of jealousy.

Even when I was at the top of my game, I could've never competed with that—with you two. With everything that you are. This is a once-in-a-lifetime moment for me. I'm honored. Deeply, deeply honored."

All cameras swivel in my direction.

Then everyone is standing. Everyone is clapping. For me, for Hamlet, for us. I'm hoping—somehow, some way—that the sound reaches you.

Hamlet scoots a little closer to the tip of my tail, leaning in. *Huh?* he says. Only it sounds like: *Would you look at this? Would you look at what we've done?*

My heart is a mouse heart and yet it's bigger.

It's thrumming.

I beam.

I—

"Clementine?" Pop says. "Would you like to say a few words, little mouse? Thank you, Gus. Yes, here's the alphabet book, here it is, if you'd like to hop on so we can—"

Crash!

A loud noise. A sound.

Heads turn. Eyes narrow. There's a gasp or two.

Beyond the cameras, the researcher has stumbled onto the set. Pretzels and pies topple to the grass as he knocks by the food table, and he's coming closer, closer.

The side of his shirt is ripped. He's splotched with tomato sauce, and—

"*I*," Gus reads, voice high, as I flit across the letters.

"*W*," Ginger chimes in loudly.

"*I*," says Mei.

"*L-L*," adds Marty, who starts advancing toward the researcher, like he's preparing to tackle him.

Pop puts it together as security floods the set. "*I will . . . G . . . Give . . . I will give . . .*"

"*Give you . . .*" Gus reads.

"*My . . .*" Pop says.

Then he stops. Everyone stops. No one is reading the rest of it out loud.

Still zooming, still flashing, I watch as all the color drains from Gus's face. Hamlet whips his head back and forth, from the researcher to me. *Huh*, he's saying frantically. *Huh?*

Gus shakes his head. "No, Clementine, *no*. You don't have to do this."

I peer up at them. At these humans.

Say it, I tell them with my eyes. *Say it, please.*

Several long seconds pass before Pop sucks in a breath, his mustache trembling and his whole face paling. "*I will give you my life.*" Emotion overwhelms his words as he reads. "*But . . . you must . . . set the others free.*"

My life, Rosie. My life is mine.

And this is what I'm choosing to do with it.

"No!" Gus screams, lurching forward. *"No!"*

But Pop holds him back, both hands on his shoulders. "Shhh, shhh, shhh," he says, voice breaking. "I know. I know. It's ripping my heart out, too."

Carefully, nervously, my paws step off the alphabet book. I pick my way past the chessboards, down the chair—toward the researcher, heart beating. I have always had a heart beating beneath the fur.

Wait, Hamlet squeaks. *Wait!* He's following me. He's coming with me.

And I tell him, *No, no, no—it'll just take one of us. It'll just take me.* But Hamlet rushes up, grabbing one of my hind paws and drawing me back to him. *Together*, he says. *Together.* So we walk together, our tails dragging through the grass, our chins held high.

We may never reunite, Rosie. You and I may never be together anywhere except these letters. Yet, there are still sunflowers blooming inside us.

You need to let yours grow.

Always,

Clementine

Letter 42
Attachment

Extract from the *Whisper Creek Gazette*

THE QUEEN'S SACRIFICE

For readers unfamiliar with a queen sacrifice in chess, a player may choose to give up their queen for the sake of the game as a whole. They lose their queen but gain a tactical advantage. This has been seen, most notably, in Byrne's 1956 game against Bobby Fischer, and in Carlsen vs. Karjakin at the 2016 World Chess Championship. It's a trade-off. A high-stakes maneuver.

Never have the stakes been higher than today. If you watched this week's episode of *Pop's Hobbies*, you know what I mean. Two superintelligent mice named Clementine and Hamlet offered *themselves* as sacrifices for the good of the game. Except this time, "the game" was the lives of others.

Letter 42

Dear Rosie,

Did you hear? Do you know that I'm alive?

They must've talked about it in the lab! They must've scrambled around, like Hamlet and I did in the maze. I can just imagine them! Watching the broadcast over and over. Trying to figure out what to do.

I should fill you in on what happened afterward.

After I hopped down from the chess table, after Hamlet followed.

Our hind paws parted the grass as we inched forward together. And finally, we were at the base of the researcher's feet. Tomato stains splotched the tips of his shoes, and he was so tall from that angle. Monstrously tall. As Gus whimpered in the background, I took one last look at Hamlet, who—in return—gave me his last *huh*. One of his paws reached out to smooth the fur beside my whiskers, as if he knew that meant something. To be groomed by another mouse. To feel. We'd started this together and we'd finish this together, side by side, tail by tail.

A mild squeak escaped me. I was determined to save you, Rosie. To let you see the sky. To let you be an Outside Chimpanzee.

But I was also very afraid.

Here's what I expected: for the researcher to bend down and pick us up by the tails. We'd dangle there, squealing, hearts pounding, before he'd toss us back into the cage. The tiny cage, with barely any room for sun.

Yet . . . a quarter of a second passed.

Then another quarter of a second.

Then the researcher bent slowly to his knees. He still had the wrinkled plum face, but it was softer somehow. Like he'd seen the sun, too. "I didn't . . ." he began, voice shaky. He took off the ice cream hat. "I didn't . . ."

Hamlet and I exchanged a quick glance, our eyes immensely wide.

What was happening?

Why weren't we dangling by our tails?

"I didn't think you could feel like *that*," the researcher finished, hands on his knees. "You were supposed to be . . . like a machine. Just a machine. I thought I was doing the right thing, but . . ." He hiccuped once. It was very loud.

Hamlet and I jumped in unison, holding on to each other. My toes pressed into his back. His ear smushed against my ear.

That's when the researcher began to cry. He bent over, his nose almost touching the grass, and he let himself rock back and forth, gently sobbing. Tentatively, Hamlet tiptoed up to the researcher, sniffed him, then patted him on the shoulder. *There. There.* It seemed like a good idea (Hamlet has many good ideas!), so I did the same, placing a paw on the creamy white of his shirt. Patting. Patting. *Oh!*

He was looking at us.

Really looking.

Really *meeting*.

He shook our tiny paws like a chess player before a match.

"I missed . . . most of your performance," he said, voice still trembling. "But I'll watch it. The whole thing. I will."

He left with much less fanfare than he arrived: slowly, out the gate, leaving an almost imperceptible trail of tomato sauce in the grass. (You'd have to be a mouse to notice it.) And I was mostly busy noticing other things. Like Gus! Like Gus, who'd burst from Pop's arms and was skidding to his knees on the grass. "I thought . . ." he said, voice still breaking, "I thought I'd lost you both forever."

I closed the gap between us, rushing up to him, and soon Hamlet was there, with Gus, with Pop, with Ginger and Mei and Marty, and we were all in the grass together. Hearts beating.

Hearts beating, still.

The researcher clanked the gate closed. Tucked close to Gus, I watched him march away—and wondered, with a pit in my belly, if I'd changed anything else. Did my performance work completely? Would I survive? Would others from the lab come to claim me and Hamlet? What about the other animals?

When would you be free?

Oh, Rosie! Rosie, I was so nervous! The edges of my ears were shaking!

(Luckily, I needn't have worried. Things changed very quickly after that.)

Fifteen minutes after the broadcast, people began showing up outside the garden. Humans with flashing cameras. Humans from the newspaper asking about Wondermouse. It seemed like everyone in a thirty-mile radius had seen me and Hamlet on *Pop's Hobbies*, and they were all shouting our names. Did we ever play chess at the lab? Did we plan to play in any other tournaments? Were there other mice with our abilities? What about checkers? How were we at backgammon?

Questions flew.

Hamlet and I watched from the living room window. That night, a journalist from the *Whisper Creek Gazette* wrote an article called "The Queen's Sacrifice." It was about me and Hamlet! About the chess game! I'll read it to you someday. I'll remember. Pretend that a copy of the article is here with these letters . . .

Now there's more. More I have to show you.

(I am not the only one who can write a good letter.)

Always,

Clementine

Letter 43

To whom it may concern:

As you might tell from the name and return address on the envelope, I'm writing to you from the Berlin Chess Championship. I've paid quite a lot in postage to deliver this message, but I feel it's rather important. I can't stop thinking about the last player I faced.

Her name is Clementine.

She was one of your lab mice.

Now, I must say, I've encountered a lot of strange opponents in my time: ones who never spoke, ones who ate tiny sandwiches through each round, and one man who sincerely believed he was a cat. By now, you've probably had a chance to view the television program known as *Pop's Hobbies*. Its host, Kristo, is a dear friend of mine. He invited me to play on his show. I thought it would be a fun but uneventful experience.

How wrong I was.

I am changed.

Sincerely, I am. I was walking down the streets of Berlin just this morning, and I saw a little gray mouse scurrying into an alleyway. I found myself following it! Just to see what it was up to! Once you know that one animal is capable of greatness, your natural thought is that *all* animals are. So there I was, tiptoeing past the trash cans, and I found the mouse. We locked eyes. And, I must tell you, I burst into tears. I couldn't stop thinking about everything that happened to Clementine—and to the other mouse, Hamlet.

I expect that you'll be receiving many letters, as your phone seems to be down—and my email, immediately before this, bounced straight back. That clip, right at the end of *Pop's Hobbies*, when Clementine hops down from the table, has been shared almost one million times! I suppose you know that. I suppose it terrifies you.

Good.

Very small regards,

Agnes Rota

Letter 44

From Gus to the lab

Dear lab people,

My name is Gus and I'm eleven years old. Last week, I found two mice in my grandpa's mailbox, and they started living next to my bed. I think they were happy there. They still are. I can tell because sometimes one of them will roll over on his back, and I can pet his belly and he giggles. The other one stays up late with me and plays chess, and we eat noodles together. I don't think that unhappy mice would do that.

They have names, you know. Clementine and Hamlet.

I used to think that "having a mind of your own" was a bad thing—but now I realize it can be good. A mind *should* be your own. Clementine helped teach me that.

She also taught me that some things are worth fighting for, even when it's difficult. So I'm going to stand up for her, and Hamlet, and the chimpanzee. I saw the way

Clementine looked at the TV when her friend came on the news. You're just being mean. Pop says that I shouldn't call people mean . . . but you're a meanie.

FREE THEM ALL!

Not sincerely,

Gus

Letter 45

From Ginger, Marty, and Mei to the lab

Greetings and salutations,

We've been debating for the last twenty minutes over who should write this letter, but I have the best handwriting, with the curly *q*'s—I've been practicing for the last ninety years—so I won. As I always do in the end. Ha! The name's Ginger, and one of you may recognize me from Fancy Fruit Supermarket on Anderson Street. I was the blue-haired beauty with the cane? On the motorized cart? Remember? Oh, what I wouldn't give to see your face right now, all splotched with tomatoes again!

Mei's telling me that I should hurry things along and this letter isn't really about me at all. Marty concurs. But who cares what Marty says, huh? Anyway.

Here's our point.

You're all a bunch of rotten, no-good nincompoops.

Mei's saying that's *not* our point. She's taking over now, apparently. Apparently, I can't be trusted. Apparently—

Hi, I'm Mei. I'm going into the sixth grade this year. Gus is a friend of mine. You've probably gotten a letter from him already. Ginger is a friend of mine, too, but she's a different type of friend. We're all really worried about the mice in your lab, the ones who got really smart in your experiment. I learned there are six. Six feels like a lot of smart mice to have around.

Gus told me there are beagles as well. And guinea pigs. And I saw the chimpanzee on TV.

It's so, so, so, so, so unfair.

That's not even enough so's.

Can't you let them out? Please? Please? Please? (That's one please from each of us.)

Thank you,

Mei, Marty, and Ginger

P.S. I have been accused of being a "letter hogger," as if "hogger" is even a word! This is Ginger again, by the way. Just so we're clear.

P.P.S. You might also receive a separate letter from Marty claiming that—from 1994 to 1997—he was the true chess champion of our little club. Believe no such thing.

P.P.P.S. I can't stop laughing about those TOMATOES!

Letter 46

From Pop to the lab

Dear Friends,

For the past seven years, I've presented a children's television program called *Pop's Hobbies*. My garden is just twelve short miles away from your lab. I think that, if we met, we'd have a great deal in common. Since I moved to this country, Whisper Creek has been my favorite home.

As I'm sure you know, six days ago, my grandson, Gus, found a pair of mice in our mailbox. They are two of the most extraordinary friends I've ever known. Clementine is optimistic, intelligent, and kind. Hamlet is a gentle companion. Because of them, I've seen Gus grow in the most wonderful ways. *I've* grown in the most wonderful ways.

Isn't it amazing? How two little mice could do that?

Now, I'd like to tell you a story.

A few years back, some of my flowers went through a rough spell, and I had to prune all the dead spots. I trimmed and trimmed, until only the fresh green was left. That way, the plants could be healthy again. I'm asking you, from the bottom of my heart, to do the same. Search inside yourselves, and see where the dead spots are, where the darkness is. And then try to prune it. Make room for something to grow in the light.

Everyone is capable of being a good friend. You showed that when you let Clementine and Hamlet go. Now it's time to be a good friend to the others, don't you think?

Warmest,

Kristo "Pop" Konstantopoulos

Letter 47

Dear Rosie,

After the broadcast, letters started to arrive, first by the bundle and then by the sackful. They tumbled from the newly repaired mailbox—no longer enough space for a mouse.

"Got another one from Canada!" Ginger liked to croon from the armchair as she sorted through a pile and fed me grapes. "And another one! You two must be the most popular mice in the world. See that, Clementine? Apparently, we're big on something called 'the YouTube.' No way they'll put you back in a cage now! Looks like that lab is getting *tons* of letters. Way more than us. Bet they're not the nice kind of letters, though. Not like ours."

When mail began spreading to all corners of our living room, rippling over the floor, the chess club took shifts. Mei is a very fast reader. So is Marty. Gus likes to spend time with each letter. Pop tries to respond to every one he reads, slipping sprigs of lavender into the envelopes alongside his replies.

Two days passed.

Two and a half.

Three.

On the third night, Pop remembered something. "My Gus!" he said. "Do you recall the opening credits from my show, from the first few episodes?"

"Yeah?" Gus said.

Pop raised his eyebrows.

"Oh!" Gus said, catching on to something. *"Oh."*

The next morning, Gus told me he had a surprise. "The terrarium's kind of cramped," he explained. "Everyone thought that you and Hamlet might need something bigger from now on. You can stay here and I can visit you every week. Or you can live with me and Pop can visit us. We'll figure it out! But . . . I'll show you! It's really cool!"

He carried Hamlet and me downstairs, where Pop was waiting, alongside . . .

What is that?

"Here," Gus said, placing us on a large platform in the shade of a tree. Except . . . the tree was my size, Rosie. On the tips of my toes, I could brush the top branches; they were crinkly like paper.

"It's my garden," Pop confirmed, "but miniature! We

used this to shoot the opening credits years ago. I dug it out of the attic last night—just for you, little mouse. Everything's to scale. Everything's there. Even some gardening tools."

"My favorite part's the tomatoes," Gus said. "They're so little!"

He held one out to me. I grabbed it from his hands and bit into it.

"Oh, that's not—"

Pew! No, not good.

Hamlet decided to try one as well, and thought that the plastic had potential.

"Go on!" Gus urged, a bit giddy. "Have a look around."

So we scurried around, flitting through the pathways, faux gravel under our paws. Everything had a label tucked into the earth.

APPLE ORCHARD.

PUMPKIN PATCH.

SUNFLOWER FIELD.

Paper flowers grew from dark soil. Trails curved by a small wooden gazebo. My tail could wrap three times around each of the dogwood trees. DOGWOOD, one of the labels said. CRAPE MYRTLE said another. That tree had magnificent pink blooms, the color of bubble gum. Near the edge of the platform, I stopped by a miniature version of Pop's house: bright windows, white shutters.

"Look inside," Gus said. "Through the window. Yep, the downstairs one. Can you see Pop? There's a drawing of him in the kitchen. And a little chess set on the counter."

Sure enough, there was.

Slowly, as we scampered around the garden, other things came into view. The impossibly small fish painted in the pond. The dimples on each miniature blackberry.

And . . .

Movement?

"It's okay," Gus said. "You can come out now!"

One by one, mice began popping out from behind trees. From behind the miniature beehive! And the tiny lettuce patch! And the mouse-size garden shed!

Not just any mice, Rosie.

Our mice. The ones from the experiment.

Hamlet skidded back on his hind paws, stunned as I was. All our whiskers pricked forward in unison. Was this real? Was this happening?

One of the mice, gray and slender, tiptoed over to us. Her paw hooked suspiciously in the air for a second—as if she wasn't sure how to say *hello*. But Hamlet dissolved any tension, barreling in. *Home!* he said, hugging them. Nestling with them. *Home, home, home.*

"The lab let them go," Gus said, a croak in his throat.

"They got *so* many complaint letters—and voice mails and angry emails and angry phone calls—and there've been people protesting outside nonstop since your chess match. Everyone said these mice should be with Wondermouse, too."

"You've made quite the impression," said Pop, rocking back on his heels. "News coverage has picked up considerably. Things are happening—oh yes. And did you know that this mouse can balance accounting books?" He pointed to a particularly tiny gray mouse near the paper mulberry bush. "The lab released them to me, and I had a box of paperwork in the car. Didn't ask him to, but this little wonder has me sorted until next tax season."

"And this one!" Gus said, reaching toward another mouse—who gently nibbled the tip of his finger. "I *think* she can read music."

I met each of them. I met them all. And it was wonderful, Rosie.

Really, it was.

But . . . where are you?

Always,
Clementine

Letter 48

Dear Rosie,

It's been forty-six seconds since my last letter.

Where are you now?

Always,

Clementine

P.S. What about now?

P.P.S. Or now?

Letter 49

From Felix to Clementine

Dear Clementine,

I'm not sure if this letter will reach you, but I hope it does! I've been doing a lot of "hoping" these days. You may not remember me. Well, you *probably* remember me. (I know that your memory is really good.) But I'm Felix! I'm the one who took you from the lab! Red hair? Kind of anxious? That's me! I would say I "freed you," but I think we both know that you freed yourself.

Anyway, a lot's happened to me since that night.

After I dropped you in that mailbox, I was so scared. So, so scared! I rushed home and cuddled my cat, Snickers, and as I sat with him on the couch, he just peered up at me like, "Buddy, Felix, my friend, what on earth are you doing?" And I *knew* he was talking about the lab. The lab kept cats once. Back in the eighties, they started with a bunch of rabbits—testing shampoo and stuff. But it's worked its way up since then. Or down, depending on how you think about it.

I quit yesterday morning. If I was willing to risk my job for a mouse, I definitely wasn't in the right career. I should've quit a long time ago.

But that's not what this letter is really about.

Before I left the lab, I read that you were good friends with a chimpanzee. A kid called Gus was talking about it to the *Whisper Creek Gazette*. Now, since there was only one chimpanzee in the lab, I'm guessing you were talking about Rosie. That's what I've been calling her for about a year. We're not supposed to give you all names (just ID numbers), but I couldn't help it with Rosie. She's pretty special, you know?

So, everyone knows your story, Clementine, but I thought you might want to know Rosie's background. She was born in the lab. She's six years old. I wish I could say that she's known the outdoors. In a better world, she would've. Her mom used to live in the lab, too, and a sister; they both got sold to another lab in Washington, DC. I wasn't there at the time. But when I read her file, it broke my heart.

Now, here's the good news.

The lab's going under, thanks to all the negative press. No one wants to work there anymore, and no one wants to fund the research. They're releasing animals left and right! Some person named Marty's adopted four of the beagles! Four! I read that in the *Whisper Creek Gazette*, too. It was the entire front page—all those dogs, just licking his face.

And Rosie! (Rosie wasn't licking his face. Sorry, I wrote that last part too fast, and now I'm wondering if I should've just crossed it out? Instead of writing this explanation?) Anyway, what I'm saying is, Rosie's being released to a sanctuary for former lab chimpanzees.

That's why I'm writing you. Would you like to see her?

Very best wishes,

Felix

Letter 50

Dear Rosie,

There once was a mouse.

That's how I began my first letter.

There once was a mouse who became friends with a chimpanzee. And now look! Look at me, thinking this letter in the back of a car. No cage in sight!

"What're you contemplating, little mouse?" Pop asks from the passenger seat of Ginger's minivan, white hair puffing in the wind. He's packed his pockets with road snacks, so his vest is wonderfully lumpy. "I've always wondered what you're thinking about, when you smell like raspberries and stare off into space like that. You cock your ears *like so*."

"Telepathy," Ginger says, tapping one of her temples—then the other temple, both hands off the wheel. "She's mind-reading *all* of us."

Gus giggles. I like it when Gus giggles. "I don't know. I think she's trying to solve something. Or remember something. Or write something. Oh! She was writing equations with the Cheerios yesterday. I felt bad because I didn't know and then I ate them. Hamlet helped."

Helped, Hamlet says, nodding next to me.

I'm here with them (Marty and Mei included), but my mind's saying *Rosie, Rosie, Rosie.* Will you still be thin when I see you? Are you afraid, where you are?

Are we there yet?

"Are we there yet?" Gus asks.

Ginger grunts. "We've been driving for less than an hour, Gus-Bus. It's still three hundred miles to the sanctuary. Hold your horses."

Horses? Hamlet asks. *Where?*

The two of us stand on each other's shoulders—him first, then me next—and peek out the window. Wind ruffles our whiskers. Rosie, where you are, I hope there's wind. I hope there's sun.

I hope you remember me.

What if you don't remember me?

We've been apart for forty-eight days. That's 1,152 hours without your chin whiskers. That's more than half my life. Yet, just as I can recall the second I was born, I can *feel* the second we met. Feel that excitement, that joy! I'm not lonely anymore, Rosie—not with Hamlet. Not with these humans and the other mice from the experiment.

But I'm still wondering if you've been counting, as I've been counting.

Did anyone tell you that you'll see me soon?

Almost. Almost.

Almost there.

The letters are there, too. Sorted and cataloged in my brain. All fifty of them, including this one. Fifty is a nice number! It's fun to say! FIF-tee! Soon, there's only fifty miles to go.

"You nervous?" Gus asks, as the van swerves down a long dirt road.

Yes!

Yes, very.

Wonderfully, wonderfully nervous.

Finally, we roll to a halt, and Gus jumps out. I'm wringing my tail in his hands. I'm glancing up at the sky, the daylight sky with all its sleeping mice—and I'm wondering if you're seeing it, too. This *same* sky, Rosie! These same flowers! Did you knuckle-walk through this door? It's swooshing open! Just like at the supermarket! Just like—

"Hello," a woman in a white coat says, greeting us in the lobby. A white coat! A lab coat? For a second, it reminds me of the researchers, and I curl up a little in Gus's hand. "Don't worry," she says softly. "I won't hurt you, Clementine."

Hamlet gives me a reassuring *squeak*. He's here. We're together.

Everything is okay.

Left! Right! Right! Down a hall! Past an office. Past a small cafeteria. Until we're bursting into the light. Before us stands a large glass window and a sign that reads VIEWING AREA.

"Go on," the woman says to Gus. "You can step a little closer."

Closer. Closer.

In the distance are tire swings and hammocks, glimmering grass and acres of leaves. There's a cool lake for dipping and ropes for jumping and trees for climbing, and oh! There! Chimpanzees! A trio of chimpanzees, tumbling down a turquoise slide. Gus lifts his palm right to the glass as I search everywhere for your face . . . and I don't see you yet. I don't see you. I don't—

Rosie.

Rosie!

You're cresting the hill, rivers of light on your fur. Your knuckles part the grass as you skip. Yes, skip! Yes, tumble! I always knew there was silliness in you. Outside, it's clear to me—clearer than it ever has been. Than it ever was. None of you was made for a cage.

I reach! I clamber! Paws against the glass, tapping it, tapping it, *Rosie!*

Rosie! Hamlet adds, raising his voice along with mine. But you're too far, still too far away, and I—

Leap! One final skitter! One final jump from Gus's hand, and I ricochet off the glass, then up the pole to the VIEWING AREA sign.

"Oh!" the white-coat woman says. "She can't . . . She can't go in there!"

But I can! I do!

I'm going.

It's a tricky route. It's tricky to fling myself from the sign, over the glass—and then climb back down the other side. But I think the flicker has caught your attention. I think you can see my movement: a small gray mouse, standing as tall as she possibly can. My whiskers whip back in the wind, but I push forward. Forward. *Rosie! Rosie!*

Are you coming? Did you catch a glimpse of me? Are you—

Footsteps!

I hear footsteps. My sensitive ears. They always know when someone is coming.

"Oh gosh," white-coat woman says behind the glass. "I don't know how this is going to go. I can't watch."

But I do.

Because your eyes are peering over the tall grass stalks. They're as kind as I remember, and even more amber in the sunlight. Do you remember me? Do you remember how you used to scoop me up, exactly as you're doing now? Do you remember how my paws would tickle the palms of your hands?

I blink.

You blink.

It's you, your eyes say, holding me close.

I nestle into you, burying my face into your chest, my tail vibrating with happiness. Black hair glittering once more, you trail a finger over the top of my head. Gently. Stroking. *Hello.* And I can hear it again, your heartbeat— your heart that is my size.

I'm ready to select the first letter now, and open it— and remember.

I'm ready to tell you about the good humans, and the chess games, and my survival.

Our survival.

Dear Rosie, I begin, whispering into you.

There once was a mouse.

> Always,
> always,
> *always*,
> Clementine

Author's Note

While Rosie is a figment of my imagination, she's based on thousands upon thousands of real chimpanzees who spent their lives trapped in laboratory cages. Thankfully, in 2015, the National Institutes of Health in the United States declared that all federally owned chimpanzees would be retired from labs. But many are still waiting for freedom.

According to Cruelty Free International, more than 115 million animals per year are subjected to experimental testing. That includes mice like Clementine and Hamlet, as well as other animals mentioned in this book: guinea pigs, rabbits, pigs, monkeys, rats, and dogs. I know a great deal about animals, and I was still shocked to learn that laboratories experiment on over 60,000 dogs per year in the United States alone.

This book was partially inspired by my childhood rabbit, Strawberry, who was rescued from a lab. She was an incredibly kind animal, and it's difficult to imagine the life she endured. Today, rabbits have become a symbol for the anti-cruelty movement. If you love animals, one of the best ways to support them is to buy cruelty-free products by looking for the Leaping Bunny logo on many household brands. Organizations like Cruelty Free International and the Beagle Freedom Project are also always eager for support.

There is hope for the future. Scientists are continuing to develop alternatives to animal testing, like replacing mice with computer models. We do not have to continue the old methods forever. Millions of animals just like Clementine are waiting for a new day.

Acknowledgments

Always, Clementine wasn't an easy book to write. None of them are easy, of course, but I was particularly anxious to get this one "right." Luckily, I have a whole team behind me.

That includes you. Yes, you! Thank you for taking the time to read this book about animals. If you've read *I, Cosmo* or *Leonard (My Life as a Cat)*, thank you for that, too. Your support means the absolute world to me, and I'm incredibly happy to have met so many of you this year through virtual school events.

To my agent, Claire Wilson: ten books later and I'm still floored that I get the opportunity to work with you. You're not just an outstanding agent—you're an outstanding human being. Thank you. And thank you to Safae El-Ouahabi and everyone at RCW.

To my editor at Nosy Crow, Tom Bonnick: I sincerely cherish our conversations. You are a wise ray of sunshine, and I always look forward to your editorial notes. You make me an infinitely more polished writer—and a braver one, too. To Susan Van Metre at Walker Books US: I am so grateful for your kindness and attention to Clementine. She is really, really fortunate to have you in her corner. Thank you as well to the teams at Nosy Crow and Walker, who have been tireless advocates for Cosmo and Leonard as well.

I cried when I saw the cover for *Always, Clementine*, illustrated by Vivienne To. Vivienne, I'm blown away by your talent. Thanks to you and Maya Tatsukawa for bringing her to life. To every bookseller, teacher, and reviewer who has championed my books: I couldn't have this career without you. Ellen Locke, Grandma Pat, Sandy Johnson, and Miss Kim—you are brilliant, supportive people. Erin Cotter, thank you for your early insight; it was invaluable! To Justin Minick at Dirty Bird CrossFit: ca-caw! You helped get me through my day, which helped get me through this book.

To Anya Taylor-Joy and everyone involved in *The Queen's Gambit*: you reignited my love of chess.

To my husband, Jago: thank you for all the future dogs we will adopt, and the rescue farm you've promised me. (That's how this works, right?) As I'm writing these acknowledgments, we've been together for ten years, and you still make me laugh every day. To my father-in-law, Chris, who has always been encouraging.

Dany! My dingo! My Soul Dog! I love you, little noodle. Lucy! Same goes for you. Bella and Duncan! Same goes for you. Thank you for all your furry snuggles and affectionate head-bops. I couldn't ask for better office companions.

For Dad, who stops his car for turtles: thank you for loving animals fiercely and for raising me in an environment where I could love them fiercely, too. And Mom, for listening. I read you this book, piece by piece, over the phone. I can't really imagine writing another way. You and Dad are true patrons of the arts.

Finally, to Strawberry, who deserved more.

About the Author

Carlie Sorosiak is the author of several books, including the novels *I, Cosmo* and *Leonard (My Life as a Cat)* and the picture books *Everywhere with You*, illustrated by Devon Holzwarth, and *Books Aren't for Eating*, illustrated by Manu Montoya. She lives in Georgia with her husband and their American dingo.